CLERICAL ERRORS

An utterly gripping cozy crime mystery

D.M. GREENWOOD

Theodora Braithwaite Murder Mysteries Book 1

JOFFE
Ostara
CLASSICS

Revised edition 2023
Joffe Books, London
www.joffebooks.com

First published in Great Britain in 1991
by Headline Publishing

This paperback edition was first published
in Great Britain in 2023

Cover art by Sasha Alsberg

ISBN: 978-1-80405-773-5

To my mother and father in gratitude

CHAPTER ONE: SCENES FROM CLERICAL LIFE

The Dean adjusted his World War Two sidecap on his bald head, wriggled his fingers inside his khaki mittens, gripped the handles of the heavy wooden wheelbarrow and broke into a trot to keep up, as it led him down the garden path towards his beloved compost heap. His fat, black Labrador bitch waddled after him, smiling.

Julia Smith, on her way to be interviewed at the diocesan office, saw him and wondered whether she should say good afternoon to a cathedral gardener. She compromised by smiling at the wheelbarrow. For the fourth time in fifteen minutes she glanced at her watch. At the same moment the pleasant light baritone of the Cathedral clock in its newly restored frame tolled the three-quarter. One forty-five.

'Canon Wheeler is in residence this month, so his diary is rather full,' his secretary had said. But he could spare her twenty minutes on Friday afternoon. 'He would be obliged if she were to attend at two' had been her precise words. Julia had relished that 'obliged if she were to attend'. Was that, then, how they communicated with each other in the Church of England? And what, she wondered, would the Canon be like? In his sixties, desiccated, with a sensible wife and the correct number of children or even grandchildren? What exactly was a 'Canon'? What did Canons *do*? Julia was nervously aware of how little she knew about the Anglican Church. She quickened her pace past the light honey-coloured west front of the Cathedral and for a moment its beauty sedated both her nervousness and that misery which was her constant, almost physical, companion.

On the other side of the Cathedral's west door, Mrs Thrigg, with a hoover, industrial model, was running its nozzle over the famous St Manicus tomb to which until quite recently, *circa* 1520, pilgrims had come to be healed: mental derangement had been the saint's particular concern. Mrs Thrigg swung the nozzle to and fro over the decorously pleated stone cassock of the recumbent saint. It paused a fraction of a second longer than was necessary in the area of the stone girdle and then darted away towards the neatly stylised beard. In and out of the ringlets went the nozzle, round his austere chaps, to end with a triumphant hiss down the mitre. Mrs Thrigg switched the instrument off with her foot, propped herself up, sweating and panting, on the cold stone and in a friendly fashion massaged the bare marble toe of the venerable old man. There were times when she felt a fellow feeling with him.

In St Manicus house opposite the north side of the Cathedral, in his office no bigger than a good sized cupboard, Ian Caretaker ground his fourth Celtique since lunch into the ashtray and massaged his ears with his hands to keep out the baritone of Canon Wheeler's well-taught voice as it seeped up from downstairs through the partly open door.

'If you didn't know Wheeler was such an ignorant ass that voice would convince you.'

'What would it convince you of?' inquired his companion in an exact, donnish tone. She was a slim woman of about twenty-seven who wore a deaconess's cross round her neck. Not without grace — for standing up she was six foot one — she uncoiled herself, took up a couple of files and edged carefully round the lethal metal points of the filing cabinet. She had no difficulty in clearing the wastepaper basket as she slid back the door of the attic room.

Ian answered her belligerently. 'That's his trick, don't you see? He doesn't have to be convincing about anything. He's just convincing in general while the sound is switched on. If you can switch the sound off and merely watch the face and figure, you get the full blast of his bogusness.'

'Most uncharitable,' said the deaconess grimly and, with a swish of her blue skirt, was gone.

* * *

'Canon Wheeler will see you now,' the light cultivated voice of the immaculate secretary said graciously. Julia, who found herself sweating, thought the secretary added 'if you would step this way' but she wasn't sure. She pushed her fringe of fair hair off her forehead and prepared to follow the slim back and trim heels of the secretary. In her dark green shirt and brown linen skirt, Julia looked a good deal cooler than she felt: at nineteen this was the first time she had been interviewed for a job. Rising from the low wooden bench in the black and white marble paved hall, she mounted the shallow-stepped staircase as it curved up to the first floor.

The heavy panelled door with its brass lock swung open and Julia saw what looked to her like a stage set, so perfect was it in every detail. The room, a double cube with four sash windows facing her, had a light filigree Adamesque plaster ceiling, a later addition but one which admirably fitted it. Very far away to her right, over several acres of silvery lilac rug, was an enormous desk. On the wall behind it hung a 6 foot-square painting of the flaying of Marsyas, a contemporary copy of the Masaccio. Below the painting was the splendid figure of Canon Wheeler, his dark-brown hair cut that morning in London, his light-grey silk suit and white shirt supporting an Oriel College tie. He wore a clerical collar when it was appropriate to do so and not when it was not. Interviewing a second secretary was a secular occasion. He knew about such matters.

Julia was quite pretty. This was apparent to Canon Wheeler when she was a quarter of the way down the first cube. As she approached, he rose elegantly to his full height of six foot three. Had she not been pretty, he would not have got up.

'How very good of you to come so promptly,' he said, his voice full tenor now rather than baritone.

Julia allowed her eye to rest for a moment on the display of Italian pornography behind Canon Wheeler's chair. By some trick of positioning the Canon seemed to be part of the picture; indeed, he stood in for Marsyas. Julia smiled, blushed, bowed her head but said nothing.

She'll do, thought Canon Wheeler and, having decided on that, he saw no reason to waste time asking tedious questions about shorthand speeds or past experience which might have involved him in listening to answers. Instead, having indicated that she might sit down, he launched into the lecture he was preparing for the Chapter meeting that evening on the necessity of hiring a new appeals fund secretary for the Cathedral restoration fund, particularly since the Diocesan Secretary was on a business studies course and the Cathedral Comptroller had recently died — Canon Wheeler's tone managed to suggest someone was to blame for this.

Though she did not quite see the relevance of the speech to the present situation, Julia, practised in receiving the opinions of others, gave him her full attention. She was appreciative, deferential.

The code words fell from the Canon's lips. 'High-powered . . . high-flyer . . . immensely able . . . professional competence . . . amateurs . . . a bit out of their depth . . . the Bishop . . . Lord Cumbermound.' Canon Wheeler's peroration effortlessly suggested the total ineptitude of everyone else with whom he had to deal and his own incisive efficiency.

Julia nodded like an old friend. While engaged in this bit of play-acting, she gradually became aware that seated unobtrusively to Canon Wheeler's right with her back to the window was a tall woman in blue wearing a cross round her neck, who was not listening to Canon Wheeler. Indeed she was looking at Julia in a detached but intent way which Julia suddenly found rather frightening. Every now and again she made a note on one of the files which she had propped on her lap. Julia speculated nervously as to who she could be. Not a secretary. Perhaps an assistant, a second opinion on her suitability? She dare not, however, remove her attention for too long from Canon Wheeler.

'Well now,' said Canon Wheeler at last with immense kindness, 'we've asked you a great many questions. I wonder if there is anything you'd like to ask us?'

Julia thought of questions she would like to ask about duties and hours, pay and holidays. She drew breath.

'I think you've covered everything very fully,' she murmured.

'Jolly good,' said Canon Wheeler jovially. 'We'll expect you, then, on Monday. The office hours are nine to five but I like my secretaries in a bit earlier to get a head start. Shall we say eight thirty?'

'Yes,' said Julia, then added, 'Thank you.' She wondered about adding 'sir', decided it might sound ironic and so did not. She need not have worried. No flattery was too gross, no praise too lavish, no hyperbole too lofty, no deference too servile, as Ian Caretaker was wont to intone in his favourite litany, for Canon Wheeler.

As she backed out, Julia heard the burble of a very modern telephone in the adjacent office and the voice of the expensive secretary, nicely poised between deference and contempt, saying, 'Canon Wheeler's office.'

Archdeacon Baggley gazed down the huge staircase of the Archdeaconry in alarm. Above him the Soane lantern cast interesting lighting effects, even with the crude afternoon sun of early July; below him was the polished greenish-brown stone floor of the hall, with its four doors very tall and dark against the white panelling. The telephone pierced the silence. The Archdeacon crept downstairs, hugging the very edge of the carpet treads. He scurried across the stone floor, deferentially skirted the tall long-case clock, grappled with the majestic door, scanned the enormous bare room and darted towards the marble fireplace. The caryatids which supported the mantel shelf did not smile at him. The Archdeacon felt himself to be a small man in more ways than one, and never smaller than when trying to inhabit his large handsome house, or when trying to reach his telephone on the high mantel shelf.

A little breathless, he raised the heavy old-fashioned black plastic to his ear a second after it had ceased to ring. With relief (no demand was to be made on him), with disappointment (an opportunity for interaction with a fellow human being was lost), he dropped the receiver back on to its rest.

'Dick?' His wife's voice was far off. He heard it gladly.

'Duckie?' he answered and trotted across the hall to the bottom of the stairs. Happily he mounted towards the beloved voice. When he was halfway up, the telephone began to ring again.

A minute later, in the Cathedral's crypt office another phone rang, a modern sound, incongruous amongst the stunted arcading. Before it had completed its first ring, a white-gloved hand raised the receiver.

'Yes.'

'Two.'

'After Compline.'

'As you wish, my lord.'

Gently the receiver clicked into place once more.

* * *

Julia heard the scream and felt first embarrassment and then a tremor of fear. She had entered the Cathedral in search of a quiet spot to collect herself after the strenuous attentiveness of her interview. She felt exhausted and headachy. Now she had got the job (what job, what would she be expected to do?) she wondered whether she really wanted it. Was any organisation which would employ her worth working for? Still, she couldn't exactly choose. She had precisely no office experience, just a three-month crash course at a secretarial college which had supplied her with barely adequate shorthand and a reasonable forty-a-minute for typing. She had had the idea that the Church might provide a fairly gentle introduction to office practice. Just in case, Julia thought morosely, she had to spend years of her life at it.

The Cathedral into which she had wandered calmed and refreshed her. She had, she realised, never entered an English Cathedral before: a childhood in Australia had given no opportunity; an adolescence in the English midlands no inclination. Her eye followed (she learned from the guidebook) clerestory to triforium and then was carried up the pale gold walls toward the narrow springing stone ribs of the roof. Tiny blue and gilt bosses joined the spokes like punctuation marks. Julia sat wedged against a tubby pillar and rested content in the coolness and the silence. This at least was something tangible which the Church could offer her. She began to feel that this holy place might perform its ancient healing work on her too: comfort for her immediate and particular misery, regeneration from a fragmented and awkward childhood. All might come right in this place.

So Julia had reflected. Hence the scream, when it came, failed to register. But it was repeated again and again with greater shrillness and violence. Now, as she heard the screaming turning to hysteria, she shuddered at the way in which the high note connected with the pain in her head. Her instinct was to run out of the building but somehow it did not seem possible to leave a fellow human being in such distress. No one else was about.

The screaming was coming from the St Manicus chapel off the Cathedral's south aisle. With measured and reluctant haste Julia turned in its direction, some ancient inhibition preventing her running in church. As she came round the corner, she saw a fat middle-aged woman holding on to the edge of the font at the back of the chapel. The hose of a vacuum cleaner was coiled round her feet like the serpent at the foot of the Tree of Life. The font, Julia registered numbly, was of white marble, floridly carved. On the edge of its ample basin was a large round object which she at first took to be a parcel. A moment later she realised that what she was staring at was a man's severed head. She was hardly conscious of the tolling of the single bell which signalled the call to three fifteen Choral Evensong.

CHAPTER TWO: ALTERNATIVE RELIGIONS

The immense sky became first silver and then pale washed-out blue as the sun rose behind Medewich Cathedral's east end, warming the splendid glass of its lancet window. It was difficult, at first sight, to understand why there was a cathedral at Medewich at all. It stood on low-lying meadows beside the Mede, surrounded by fens for ten miles in three directions. The founder, St Manicus, in the twelfth century (his statue came two hundred years later) had taken refuge there from the civil disturbances of the time. Driven from his property by his relations, he had, for a time, lost his reason and thought he heard voices. Wandering in his demented state, he had arrived one day at the hamlet of Medewich. There, amidst its dank and mosquito-infested ponds, his voices vanished and the madness departed. In gratitude, he built a small chapel with his own hands, the St Manicus chapel, and, framing his own rule, lived the life of a monk.

In time, others had joined him and the house became an established centre, famed for medical cures, especially of the insane. However, in his seventieth year, Manicus had had his head chopped off by a madman whose delusion it was to consider himself an executioner. His fellow monks, lamenting his demise, buried Manicus and his head in the chapel and were not at all surprised when various miracles of healing were reported. A literary monk with journalistic gifts and a nice Latin style turned out a neatly phrased piece of hagiography and sent it off to Rome. Various interests combined (the Earl of Medewich and Markham knew a sound thing when he saw it) and Manicus was canonised a mere ten years after his appalling end.

Pilgrims had come with their money and madnesses and a cathedral had been built. Manicus, though never a bishop, came to be regarded as one, hence his later statue which showed him mitred. After the Reformation, though madness had doubtless not disappeared, pilgrims did. In the eighteenth century, local interests combined with Dutch expertise to practise elementary and expensive draining techniques which had rendered some of the surrounding land less boggy. Otherwise Medewich's remoteness had preserved both Cathedral and town from every appearance of modernity until, in the nineteenth century, the Earl of Medewich and Markham of the time had lured the railway across his land with a view to conveying fish more speedily from the coastal harbour of Narborough to the London market. A station had been built at Medewich and the unspoilt charms of the Cathedral, with its bizarre legend and curious atmosphere, had attracted its share of late nineteenth-century antiquarians. At that time too, the barracks, the lunatic asylum and the prison had all been added. Designed, the first two in an austere classical style and the asylum, in the Gothic taste, by a pupil of Street, they stood within sight of each other to the north of the town, looking down on the Cathedral, a holy trinity dedicated to order, sanity and retribution.

Julia woke with the rising sun from unhappy dreams and gazed towards the lunatic asylum. She had refused the sedatives which she had been offered by the young doctor called to the chapel. Called to do what? Julia wondered. Hardly, surely, to issue a death certificate for the head. She had spent what seemed like hours answering police questions in the vestry of the Cathedral before refusing the offer of a police car home. She had walked back in the late evening through the silent, handsome town to her lodgings up the hill. There, slipping into and out of nightmares in which the identity of the severed head had grown more and more familiar to her, she had lain until dawn.

Her first feeling this morning was that she didn't want the diocesan office job. Her next was that her finances were so low, her prospects so diminished that really she did not have too much choice. Moreover, she was curious. Julia thought she detected a complete and separate world in the Church of England. Nor did she think that that world looked as though it very much resembled the one depicted by Trollope. Julia collected worlds, having none of her own. She knew nothing of Anglicanism. What would that world make of an invasion of madness and violence? A severed head in a font. Could sacrilege have any place still in the modern, secular age? It would be intriguing to see if it did. What would she discover? Julia wondered, as she gazed through the open window of her bedroom.

Moreover, Julia reflected, Medewich was beautiful and her room, in the attic of an early nineteenth-century terrace, a luxury. If the nineteenth century had built a university instead of the barracks, prison and asylum, Julia thought, she wouldn't have got accommodation so easily. Her mind jumped to the misery of her last room in Cambridge, to the poky, noisy little flat in which she and Michael had first loved and then hated each other. To banish such thoughts, she got up. Saturday meant shopping. Though she had no money, she would investigate the town and get herself equipped for the new job and a new life.

* * *

The Cathedral bell tolled for the eight o'clock Eucharist. The deaconess, on her way to service in the Cathedral, placed her shopping list inside her prayer book so that it marked the appropriate Sunday after Trinity, rolled her string bag briskly inside her capacious handbag and strode manfully across the perfect lawn which separated her lodgings in the Archdeaconry from the Cathedral's south door. There appeared to be rather more people than was usual bound for the early service, she noticed. Perhaps there had been a revival of religious enthusiasm. However, the presence of the police cars suggested a more basic psychological urge was at work in the hearts of Medewich's citizens. She paused at the small, to her always inviting, wooden door of the St Manicus chapel and reflected: blood, violence and madness, these were the foundations, after all, of every religion. She grasped the cool iron handle and plunged into the darkness beyond.

* * *

Medewich market on Saturdays was the centre of social as well as commercial life in the town. Situated below the west door of the Cathedral on cobbles which bore evidence of rotting fruit and discarded vegetables long after its closure in the evening, it was possible to buy anything there, from salad to shoes. Three main streets led down to it. Julia, wandering downhill from her lodgings, was both soothed and stimulated by its life. Edging through the already crowded aisles between the stalls, it was possible to feel a continuity with the past history of the place. Fruit and vegetables like these, local and foreign, must always have been sold here. Their smells and the soft local accent proclaiming their virtues need not have been different eight hundred years ago in St Manicus's time.

Julia wandered contentedly round the stalls until the smell of new bread reminded her that she had not eaten since yesterday's snack before the interview. She had not wanted food after the events in the St Manicus chapel. A stall selling bacon rolls and strong sweet Indian tea gave her sustenance. Holding her food and drink she made for the centre of the market and sat down on the now sun-warmed steps of the butter cross. From this slightly raised position it was possible to look toward the west door of the Cathedral. In the courtyard to the south, beside the St Manicus chapel, she could see two police cars parked. It occurred to her to wonder what the local press was making of the affair. She ceased feeding the already gross pigeons with the remains of her roll, went back for a second cup of the thick, delicious tea and bought a paper.

The *Medewich Daily Press*, unlike its stable companion, the *Medewich Evening News*, was a sober and unpopular journal which did its best to pretend it was not a local paper by taking a very high moral tone in its criticism of international men and affairs. From its front page, normally, it was not possible to find any reference to local news, though the inner pages made concessions to local interests with reports of planning decisions (always mistaken). Today, however, national affairs were relegated to the second page. A victory for a very young sub editor (taken on in last year's graduate entry from Cambridge) allowed the headlines to proclaim:

> *KILLER GHOST WALKS AGAIN*
> *SEVERED HEAD IN ST MANICUS' FONT*

> *Clergy are asking themselves whether the ghost of the murderer of St Manicus still stalks the Cathedral. Yesterday evening the dead head of a man was discovered by Mrs Miranda Thrigg, 54, of Markham Terrace, Medewich, while cleaning the font in the St Manicus chapel. 'I was completely bowled over,' said Mrs Thrigg. 'I, for one, would not be surprised if no human hand had done this deed.'*

Having won his headline and first paragraph, the sub editor had lost the battle for the rest of the story and the report continued in the normal prose style of the press.

> *It is understood that, as yet, there has been no identification of the head, which was that of a young man with red hair. Doctors estimate his height at about six foot.*

How on earth do they do that, thought Julia. The report then went on to say that the Dean and Chapter had not issued a communiqué, as yet, but the waiting world would have the advantage of that later in the day.

Julia admired the use of the word 'dead' to describe the head and the spelling of 'bold' in the report of Mrs Thrigg's quoted words. She glanced up towards the Cathedral with its tiny bump of a Chapter house on the north side. Did they all sit round in fancy dress on throne-like chairs drafting an ecclesiastical statement, she wondered. Julia had been educated at an Australian comprehensive school before her father died and then in the rather more hellish atmosphere of an English Further Education College in Wolverhampton. There, she had gained, against mighty odds, a couple of A levels in English and Mathematics which fitted her for precisely nothing. Religion in any form other than aboriginal non-conformity had played no part in her juvenile experience. Her knowledge of English and European history and literature, such as it was, derived entirely from listening to Michael and his friends at Cambridge. She felt, however, no inferiority for her lack of background, though occasionally she was mystified. She brought a fresh and observant eye to the language and institutions of her father's country and made attempts to investigate and read about whatever she found particularly baffling. On the whole she found it a stimulating experience.

'Miss Smith?'

Julia started and looked up. She found gazing down on her the very tall woman who had been present at her interview with Canon Wheeler the previous day. The woman was dressed in a plain dark-blue linen dress which was only just not a uniform. Julia got up from the butter cross steps.

'Oh, good morning. I'm afraid I don't . . .'

'Theodora Braithwaite,' said the tall woman holding out her hand.

'How do you do? I'm afraid I . . .'

'I tried to contact you yesterday evening after you'd seen the police.'

Julia's mind jumped apprehensively, irrationally. Did that mean that they were withdrawing the offer of the job? Perhaps people who were contaminated by finding severed heads in cathedral fonts couldn't be employed in cathedral offices as typists.

'I'm afraid . . .'

'I thought that perhaps you might be in need of solace. I can imagine how very unpleasant time spent with the police might be. Not to mention, of course,' she added apparently as an afterthought, 'the horridness of your discovery.'

Julia analysed this quickly. The offer of comfort was, she felt sure, genuine. So was the disdain for the police; so was the dismissal of the actual experience of finding the head. She felt reassured by this list of priorities, even if it didn't quite coincide with her own.

'It's very kind of you. The police weren't too bad. There wasn't actually much I could tell them. But they seem to like you to say everything three times rather slowly and from slightly different angles.'

Theodora looked at Julia keenly. She appeared to find the sentiments congenial.

'I'm going to see my colleague, Ian Caretaker,' she said. 'I wonder if you'd care to come and have some coffee with us?'

* * *

Julia trotted along beside Theodora feeling very much as though she had been taken charge of but not at all resenting it. They crossed the river by the traffic bridge and turned left down the tow path. Moored at the end of a long line of modern fibre glass cruisers was a long, low timber boat like a masted barge. Though rigged, the rust-coloured sail was furled along the immense boom. From the top of the mast there flew a flag which Julia recognised from her Australian youth: Thailand.

'Dhani Tambiah, my colleague Ian Caretaker's friend, owns it and Ian is lodging there for the moment,' Theodora explained.

Julia stepped aboard the boat with delight. The solidity of the old, well-maintained timbers reassured her. It smelt of tar and varnish and herbs, the herbs wafting from a galley to the for'ard where cooking of an un-English kind was going on. She followed the tall figure of Theodora aft, picking her way round coiled ropes and brass bollards. On the deck beside the tiller and beneath a canvas awning to provide shade from the now hot sun, she detected two seated figures. Dhani Tambiah — neat-figured, bronze-coloured and barefoot, like a small Buddha — was sitting in a half-lotus on the broad aft bench. He got up beautifully, without hurry, without stiffness, and gave her his hand. He looked her gently in the eye and smiled.

'How do you do?' they said together.

'You're most welcome to my home,' said Dhani. Then Ian came forward.

'May I introduce,' said Theodora formally, 'Ian Caretaker, Julia Smith.'

'Hello,' said Ian with less formality than Theodora.

'It's a beautiful boat,' said Julia warmly.

'It suits us admirably,' said Ian proprietarily.

'What is it?' Julia inquired.

'A Norfolk wherry built to carry grain round the coast. Built about 1870 by Yaxlee and Maingay of Narborough for Tallboy and Sons of Medewich. It worked until about 1950 when Tallboys' ceased trading. It has an original Crossley engine, with a lovely deep note.'

Julia, as always, was flattered by male didacticism.

'Tea or herbal tea?' said Dhani.

'Coffee,' said Theodora firmly.

'It'll do you no good,' said Dhani darkly and disappeared below deck.

'Ian is Canon Wheeler's lay assistant,' said Theodora, experimentally seating herself on a canvas chair as they all disposed themselves on the warm timbers of the deck.

'Oh, yes,' said Julia, perfectly prepared to be discreet if that should prove to be necessary. There was plenty to enjoy on this lovely boat. It was only to be expected that there should be some fly in the ointment. Ian's grin widened but also tightened.

'Theodora told me she thought you handled the egregious Canon rather well.'

'I wasn't required to do very much,' said Julia.

'That will come later,' said Ian. 'How good are you at dealing with bullies?'

Before Julia could reply, Dhani returned with a tray. Julia found herself pressed to have herb tea which was delicious and refreshing. Theodora drank coffee and Ian continued.

'They had an informal Chapter last night. They'll hold a formal one this morning to get out a press statement. The head belongs to Paul Gray of St Saviour's Markham cum Cumbermound. They're looking for his car: SVF 907 Ford Escort, diocesan issue.'

Julia put her cup down rather suddenly and made as though to speak. Theodora regarded her for a moment and then Ian continued.

'Chapter, by which I mean Canon Wheeler, who had a great deal to say, as always, seemed to indicate that they were neither surprised nor sorry that Gray had had his head chopped off. Many of his parishioners, Wheeler indicated, have had this thought in mind since he took over from the innocuous Longman at the beginning of the year. Indeed, he implied his PCC might well have been drawing lots for the honour. By the time Wheeler had finished we were surprised that the fellow had survived so long.'

'Ian, don't be so tasteless,' said Theodora crisply. 'You're shocking Julia, or at least you have no right to infect her with your cynicism.'

Julia wasn't sure whether she was shocked or not. Of the two conversational gambits open to her she chose the easier. She was, she said, rather surprised to find someone who wasn't a priest working for the Church.

'Well,' said Ian and Theodora together.

'I think,' said Ian, 'that Julia's education in such matters should come from me since I'm the only real layman here.'

Dhani smiled enigmatically.

'The Church,' said Ian, clearly launching into a prepared tract, 'is, like God, both immanent and transcendent. That is to say, as well as being the company of all faithful Christian people living and dead, it is also an institution within a temporal and historical polity.' He was enjoying himself.

Julia glanced across at Theodora while Ian was talking. The deaconess was leaning back in the chair, her face shadowed by the canvas awning. Julia was again aware that Theodora had a presence, that she was allowing Ian to perform.

'It is with the latter aspect of the church,' Ian was striding on, 'that we are concerned. It owns property, builds and maintains edifices, employs and even occasionally sacks people. That means that there are two layers of people. Priests, one per cent of the whole, who are there for ornament and to provide visible symbols of the transcendent reality acted out in liturgy. And laymen, ninety-nine per cent of the whole, who are there to support the one per cent. Every priest, therefore, needs his lay equivalent, his minder, who marshals the money, who phones the plumber, who . . .'

'Oh, really, Ian, that's quite enough,' said Theodora. 'Tell us what more you know about the murder. Julia can pick up the niceties of Anglicanism later.'

Julia said hesitantly, 'Is there anything I could read on the Church, to get the hang of it, as it were?'

'You should approach the Church of England as you might approach a wine tasting,' Ian said grandly. 'Mere information is not enough, the taste is all. I am currently working on the definitive layman's guide to the Anglican Church. It will not be published by Church House.'

The joke was lost on Julia; the others had heard it before.

'When was Gray killed?' Theodora asked Ian, dragging him back to the point.

'And, incidentally, how do you know what Chapter decided?' added Dhani.

'Which the press don't know,' finished Julia.

Ian looked pleased. 'I was acting as Wheeler's sidekick at Chapter last night — he likes to have the equivalent of an office boy or runner in attendance to send on errands and give a few orders to. In between errands I gathered that Gray was quite well known to the Chapter. Archdeacon Baggley had had no difficulty in making an identification for the police. There'd been a spot of bother in his first curacy and he was known to be one of the Bishop's favourites.'

'And he was killed, when?' asked Theodora again.

'It's apparently difficult to tell precisely from a head alone,' said Ian judiciously. 'They'll know better when, and if, they find the body.'

'Which they have not yet done,' said Theodora.

Julia noted that Theodora's and Ian's intonation and turn of phrase frequently resembled each other's. Either they knew each other well or else they had read, thought Julia, the same sort of books. Like Michael, she thought, and for a moment her world went dark.

'Why should anyone want to kill Paul Gray?' Dhani inquired.

Theodora looked at Ian. 'Do the police share Canon Wheeler's view that the murderer comes from within Gray's parish?'

'We had a little terrier of a superintendent — Frost, I think he was called — hovering at the elbow of the Chief Constable, who was clearly embarrassed by a clerical corpse. They gave absolutely nothing away. I thought that they hadn't anything to give. They've had a pair of nice Alsatians quartering the Cathedral environs this morning to see if they could turn up the actual body. A task in which they will not be helped by the amount of tar the clerk of works' men are managing to spill all over the place in their efforts to resurface the paths.'

'But why should any of his parishioners want to kill Paul — Reverend Gray?' Julia asked hesitantly.

'Communities need victims,' said Theodora thoughtfully, 'and sometimes the priest, who is both visible and often innocent, fulfils this function.' She paused. 'Although it rarely ends in murder.'

Julia was baffled. 'But why do they need a victim?' she said helplessly.

'To render the community holy, to act as a scapegoat, a focus for the hatreds it cannot otherwise deal with. We all need something we can legitimately hate.'

'A sort of madness,' murmured Dhani.

'Look at St Manicus's own murderer,' said Ian.

'Will it,' asked Julia, returning to her earlier fear, 'will it make any difference to the diocese, the office, I mean the job I was offered?'

Ian looked at her kindly. 'I don't think a thinning of the ranks of clergy means a reciprocal diminution in the ranks of laity. Rather the contrary. The fewer priests the more laity are needed. Caretaker's first law of clerical energy.'

Two mallards swam over the soupy, green water and squawked at them hopefully, and Dhani disappeared below to fetch some brown bread. The four of them fed the ducks companionably, all sense of strain dissipating rapidly. The tight look which appeared on Ian's face when he thought of Wheeler vanished and Theodora lost her rather formidable formality and showed a swift accuracy in the placing of her bread pellets.

'A skill,' said Theodora when Julia complimented her, 'perfected through five years at an English girls' boarding school.'

Julia, invited to stay for lunch, accepted gladly and they spent a cheerful meal eating a delicious vegetable stew. They were not inquisitive Julia noticed but she felt their genuine kindness and offered a little of her own background, the Australian bit, in payment. What she told them was received with interest, she felt, and to her relief, without demand for more.

Finally, as she and Theodora were about to depart, Ian made a suggestion. 'How about a trip upriver by the evening light?' he asked. 'It's a good way of learning your way round Medewich. You see all the old parts and none of the modern development. Do allow me to have that pleasure,' he added, suddenly formal.

Julia blushed a little and said she'd love to.

'Would seven thirty be a possibility?'

Julia said it would, and he arranged to pick her up, at the town quay below the west front of the Cathedral.

The two women strolled back through the town together. Although slightly in awe of Theodora, Julia was sufficiently curious to summon up courage to question her. Here, after all, was an opportunity to begin her research into the world of the Anglican Church.

'Theodora, are you a priest?' Julia judged that she should be direct.

'No. I'm in deacon's orders. One below, as it were.'

'Will you become a priest in time?'

'Not unless they change the rules about women.'

'Why shouldn't they?'

'The reasons are complicated. Some historical, some social, some, it is even suggested, are theological.'

'So,' said Julia valiantly, 'what can't you do that a priest can?'

'I can marry, baptise and bury but I can't consecrate the elements, the bread and wine, at the Eucharist, nor can I give absolution from sin.'

Julia ruminated. 'Could you ever be the vicar of a parish then?'

'Only with difficulty,' said Theodora grimly.

Theodora's tone had become rather clipped, so Julia desisted and they went on through the market. Theodora seemed to feel she'd been curt and after a moment she offered, 'Had you any particular reason for settling on Medewich for what I gather is your first post?'

Julia hesitated. She had no intention of lying and indeed no identifiable reason for concealing anything. On the other hand, Theodora, as far as she could tell, was of the employing classes. The fear of being drawn in or in some way tied down was strong in Julia.

'My father has, used to have, some relations, second cousins in the area so it seemed a good idea. I'm not sure I'll be staying long in any case.' Julia realised she'd got herself into a muddle. 'I mean, of course, it, the Church, will be valuable experience, office training . . .' She was reduced to mumbling. 'But if I'm any good I expect I'll move on in due course, after a decent interval.'

'Oh quite.' Theodora was amused rather than censorious. 'A diocesan office may well have things to offer you, though I doubt if they will pertain to sophisticated office practice. We have yet, for example, to computerise. Not a word processor to our names.'

Julia was sorry about this since her typing skills were meagre.

'However,' said Theodora, looking at her watch and turning decisively right towards the steps up to the Cathedral and Canons' Court, 'I've no doubt you'll learn something. Nothing is ever lost.'

Julia wasn't sure whether this was meant to daunt or encourage her. But on the whole she felt she'd made a good start in her Anglican investigations. Happy in her new acquaintances, she strolled back through the now less busy market and stopped at a second-hand book stall on its outskirts. Her eye was taken by a handsome history of Medewich Cathedral in a splendid blue leather binding. She had just turned the frontispiece and was gazing at the steel engraving of the west front about 1890, when her ear caught a familiar voice.

'I thought you said you'd have them ready.'

The accent was local and the tone, sharp and nervous, was familiar. Julia looked up and saw the plump form of the Cathedral cleaner, Mrs Thrigg. She was leaning forward and talking to a man of not quite English appearance whose stall it appeared to be. The trestles were piled high with cheap brass, wickerwork and potpourri. Julia was about to greet the woman when she pulled herself up short. Perhaps one would not want to be reminded of what would have been a distressing occasion. Her eye returned to the book and she bent her head over its pages. Mrs Thrigg's high-pitched harangue was more audible than her victim's response.

'I did say. I did tell you, didn't I. I said, they've got to be here before six on Saturday. We pay enough for them. I told my ladies. I said, we pay enough for them in all conscience.'

Julia moved away, letting the history of Medewich go back to its place. Slowly she began to climb up the hill to her lodgings.

* * *

Julia trailed her hand in the cool water. It was a measure of Ian Caretaker's presence that, in spite of the beauty of the evening and the river setting, she found no difficulty in keeping at bay memories of Michael and the Cambridge backs. Ian's competent form could be made out in the evening light as he moved the long, old-fashioned oars of the heavy craft dexterously through the water. He looked, she thought, like one of those drawings from *Boy's Own Paper* of about 1900. His hair was as long and neat as it would have been then and not short as the boys in Australia had been wearing it when she'd left. He wore a white shirt with long sleeves loosely rolled up and flapping, rather baggy flannels, not jeans, and scuffed canvas rope-soled shoes. A thin leather belt with the end tucked in, not slotted through a keeper, held his trousers.

The boat, built in heavy oak tarred innumerable times outside and worn to a pleasant silver colour inside, was the tender to the wherry *Amy Roy*. It sat low in the water and appeared at home in it. The whole made a harmonious picture not quite of this century.

The Mede bound the Cathedral on three sides, south, east and north, and the market and the town with its quay lay below the Cathedral's west front. The hills on which the asylum, barracks and prison were placed reared up to the north of the Cathedral. There was an elegant modern footbridge linking the Cathedral's site with the east side of the river and a traffic bridge, originally Norman, which led from just beyond the market place to the commercial docks on the south bank. The confines of the river had made modern development near the Cathedral impossible. The buildings which surrounded it, St Manicus house and the choir school to the north and the Deanery, Archdeaconry and Canons' Court to the south, with the Bishop's Palace facing the east end, made a harmonious range of buildings. Originally mediaeval, they had been modernised in 1750 and 1820.

Julia and Ian proceeded slowly past the south side of the Cathedral. The river, which continued to be a working river with coasters from Narborough as far as the town quay, began here to narrow and became purely domestic and pleasure seeking. The back gardens of the Deanery, Archdeaconry and Canons' Court sloped with perfect lawns down to the river. The three houses which made up Canons' Court shared a single garden unmarred by flower beds. The facades of these buildings fronting the Cathedral were stone-faced. Their backs, however, showed earlier picturesque layers of seventeenth-century brick, sixteenth-century ragstone and bits of dressed stone pillaged indecently from monastic buildings after the Reformation. The nineteenth century had seen drainpipes added and the early twentieth, lavatories and bathrooms built out on stilts at first-floor level. It was all highly agreeable. Julia felt that she was seeing it at the right pace, about three miles per hour, and at the right hour, near sunset, and, she realised, after an informed architectural lecture from Ian, in the right company. Her thoughts turned again to the events of the day.

'If you live in such beautiful surroundings,' she remarked to Ian when he paused in his efforts, 'surely it must be easier to be good. I mean generous and truthful. Do you think?'

'In theory, yes. But in fact, turning your collar round and convincing ACCM that God has called you seems to have an effect on the moral character so deleterious that even architectural beauty can't heal it.'

'You don't seem too keen on Christianity,' said Julia with a sudden directness. 'You choose to work for it but haven't a good word to say for it.'

'You're mistaken,' Ian replied, without roughness. 'I have no reservations at all about Christianity. It's all there is to keep the devil at bay. It's complete and true.' He spoke with passion. 'But about Anglicanism, how can one not be ambivalent? I love it dearly and you must know how close that can come to hate. Its tolerance can so easily become self-indulgence and complacency. Its kindness can turn into patronage and its easy relations with the political and social stage so quickly degenerate into worldliness and power seeking.'

'Is that why you're not a priest?' asked Julia.

'No. I haven't attained that purity of life which would entitle me to the priesthood. It's an honour. It's also a vocation and I don't have that either.'

Julia paused. 'Why do you hate Canon Wheeler?'

Ian stopped rowing for a moment. 'Perhaps because he enjoys that honour and possesses that vocation I've just been talking about.'

'And what about Dhani?' asked Julia exploring remorselessly.

'What about him?' replied Caretaker.

'What is he, religiously, I mean?'

'Religiously he's a Buddhist.'

'What do they believe?'

'Buddhism isn't, I think, a matter of beliefs so much as the adoption of certain techniques for living.'

'Such as?'

'Well, what one is aiming at, in Dhani's sort of Buddhism, is not to aim at anything. Do you see?'

'No,' said Julia with finality.

'Well, what he cultivates is a sort of relaxed alertness. A form of detached self-knowledge. A balance.'

'Why?'

'For the thing in itself.'

Julia felt herself quite out of her depth. They had drifted under the modern footbridge. She allowed her eye to travel upwards to the Cathedral's east window which by now had begun to reflect the setting sun.

'What does he make of the murder?' she asked.

'I don't know,' said Ian. 'But I think it wouldn't be important to him.'

'How can a grotesque horror like chopping off a man's — a young priest's — head and leaving it in a place people come to worship in, not move him?' said Julia with an emotion which grew as she framed the words and allowed all the revulsion which she had suppressed and left unacknowledged since the previous day to be given full rein. She was near to tears.

Caretaker stopped rowing and shipped the oars. He leaned forward and said earnestly, 'You're quite right to feel as you do. That's the Christian part. But you will also have to learn to cope with that feeling, that's the Buddhist part. Try putting the horror into your breath and sighing it, blowing it, hissing it out.'

He spoke with such conviction that Julia restrained her urge to laugh and merely smiled at him. She felt his kindness and was grateful even for something she could make nothing of.

They had drifted to the north of the Cathedral and could clearly see the first of the three Victorian buildings of prison, barracks and asylum which crowned the hill to the north.

'Shall we walk up and see the view before we start back?' asked Ian.

They walked companionably up the mixture of heathland and scrub which bounded the lower slopes of the hill. It was further than they had thought, fooled by the deceptiveness of buildings seen at odd angles from below. By the time they reached the outer periphery of the asylum's range of buildings, darkness was encroaching. The main building stretched a long way and was magnified in height by the lack of light. Its Gothic features, which in daylight looked rather parsimonious, by night took on a solidity and presence which were daunting. There was a low wall surmounted by iron railings. Not too far from where they were, an iron gate leading into the grounds stood open. Beside the main building there was a collection of more modern buildings about four hundred yards from the main block, which seemed to be derelict.

'Is the asylum still used?' asked Julia.

'In conformity with the Ministerial circulars, a policy of easing inmates who are not too dangerous or incapacitated back into the community has been initiated. I think the plan is to close it within three years. Certainly it hasn't many inmates and the out-buildings haven't been used since I came back to Medewich.'

Julia allowed herself to feel the atmosphere of the place. Her mind went too easily to the hopeless and distraught who had until recently occupied the rooms behind the blank dark windows. Slowly she turned towards the south, away from the pile of the asylum and looked towards the town and its lights. They radiated a remote but comforting normality on the marsh below them. The full moon was beginning to thicken behind the spire of the Cathedral. It struck ten. The lights on the motorway which connected Medewich with the rest of the civilised world were a dull glow to their right.

Julia thought about Ian's advice to breathe out the horror of the obscene head. She had just started to draw breath into her lungs slowly, when she heard or rather felt a thudding noise; at first she wasn't sure whether it was in her head. She turned to Ian, who had been standing looking towards the river with a relaxed air a moment before. She was surprised to find him already tense and listening alertly.

'What is it?' She found herself whispering.

'The local peasants,' said Ian, 'with a cassette player.'

'It doesn't sound like it,' Julia answered.

The sound was louder now, an insistent, taut throbbing. Julia found herself connecting the sound with a physical sensation at the base of her skull, like the beginning of a headache. The rhythm was by no means simple and, as it grew to a crescendo, her breath came in pants and she began to shake. For the second time in twenty-four hours she felt as though a sound were possessing her. She turned to Ian, her distress mounting.

'Ought we to go and investigate?'

'Probably I ought to and you ought not,' he said. 'But I've no intention of leaving you alone. Come on, let's go back to the boat.'

They started to move down the hill when suddenly there was another sound. This time it was high-pitched and either animal or human. A prolonged scream. It was swiftly followed by another. I can't bear this, Julia thought.

Ian seized her hand in his and began to run back towards the sound, plunging up the hill through the open gate towards the nearest of the two asylum out-buildings. They were within ten yards of the door when the drumming ceased. Ian, clearly determined to use the surge of adrenalin summoned by his charge up the hill to give him courage to face whatever was on the other side of the door, seemed to Julia's blurred perception of the scene to be shouting as he launched himself at the door. It did not give way to him immediately, but he kicked with unnecessary violence and it fell open. There was a rush of warm air and a faint acrid smell of smoke. It was very dark. Ian paused. Julia's eyes, by now accustomed to the dark, spotted something long and white lying on the floor towards the far end of the room. They moved cautiously towards it and Ian bent to pick it up. It was thick, slightly greasy and tubular. After a moment he realised it was nothing more than a candle, with the wick still smouldering. From far away and below came the sound of a powerful motorbike engine being revved into life.

CHAPTER THREE: OFFICE PRACTICES

'Hello, Mary. Morning, Archdeacon. Good morning, Dean. Good morning, Canon.' From her small cubby-hole on the opposite side of Canon Wheeler's office to Miss Coldharbour's room, Julia listened to Theodora's litany with interest. It was the third day she had heard it. Wednesday. The intonation never varied and was nicely calculated. To Mary, the receptionist, brisk; to the Archdeacon, comradely; to the Dean, friendly; to Canon Wheeler, deferential. They all worked with their doors open in the early part of the morning. Whether this was because of the weather, which was warm, or because they were all as curious as cats or, perhaps, because they were actors manqué, Julia had not yet decided.

The layout of the original house had not been much altered and there was a pleasing absence of fluorescent lights and plastic furniture. A back staircase, originally for servants, ran from ground-floor level to attics and was entered from a door to which Ian, Theodora and the clergy had keys. It was handy since it opened directly on to the parking slots for office staff, much prized and intrigued over. The lower orders were denied the privilege of the back door and entered through the front. However, on one's first appearance in the office in the morning it was etiquette for all, even key holders, to enter through the front door and use the front staircase. On their way up to their office in the attic, therefore, Ian and Theodora had to pass the open doors of the offices of the Dean and the Archdeacon on the ground floor, and that of Canon Wheeler on the first. Ian got in earlier than any of the clerics and so avoided the business of greetings. Theodora got in exactly at nine every day and punctiliously greeted whoever of the clergy were in at that hour.

In the course of her first couple of days, Julia found the social nuances of the office a constant source of surprise. Unfamiliar as she was with the niceties of English social life, she wondered why she should be surprised. What, after all, had she expected in the Church of England in a provincial town a hundred miles from London and the Midland conurbations? But the formality and hierarchical nature of the relationships still struck her. To each other, what Julia had heard Canon Wheeler describe as 'the senior clergy' were comradely in a slightly country cricket club way. They employed Christian names rather than titles but their turns of phrase for communication with each other, whether written or spoken, were formal in all cases and on occasions orotund.

'Gerald, I wonder if I might trespass on your good nature?' Julia incredulously heard the Archdeacon say to the Dean, the tone, which was mellifluous, floating up the elegant staircase.

On the other hand, their subordinates — that large body of laymen and women who, as assistants or typists, seemed necessary to support what Ian had called the one per cent — addressed these senior clergy by their titles to their faces and even amongst themselves referred to their superiors in this way. At first, Julia had suspected irony but, though she had listened carefully, she did not think, as yet, that she detected any. They were taken, then, were they, these clergy, at their own evaluation? Nothing in Australian society nor in the easy commerce between don and undergraduate which she had witnessed and occasionally shared with Michael at Cambridge, had prepared her for this. The superiority conferred by money or that of being an expert in a field she had glimpsed and credited, but on what, she wondered, apart from their rank, did the superiority of these senior clergy rest? Was it, perhaps, that they were of higher moral virtue than other men? Julia set out to test this hypothesis. She thought, child of an experimental scientist that she was, that she would make the test for herself and not take the easy way out of asking those experts in all matters Anglican, Theodora and Ian.

It looked as though at least some progress in that experiment might be able to be made soon. It was apparent to Julia that her work was poor. The secretarial course had been very much a crash one. She lacked experience and had no one to advise her. Her typing was slow and riddled with mistakes, the layout eccentric. The first secretary, Miss Coldharbour, Canon Wheeler's immaculate conception, as Ian called her, had on the first day coolly returned Julia's first batch of letters with mistakes marked in a soft shorthand pencil which proved difficult to eradicate cleanly with a rubber when the corrections had been made. The finished effect was grubby. Miss Coldharbour had glanced at them fastidiously, scarcely concealing a shudder. The same thing happened the following day. Julia felt she might not make the end of the week if this went on. Her, never great, self-confidence was oozing away. She wondered if Miss Coldharbour had the power to sack her or whether she would simply recommend this course of action to Canon Wheeler. Julia resolved to double-check everything she typed today and stay late, if need be, to get up to date. The amount of work was formidable. The idea that a diocesan office might be a gentle or leisurely introduction to office practice was wide of the mark.

She sorted out the in-tray left for her by Miss Coldharbour: audio tapes for Canon Wheeler, drafts for Miss Coldharbour and a plain manilla folder marked 'urgent'. She opened it and read the note on top.

I require two copies of this by noon today.
Wednesday 8 July. CVW.

Julia glanced at the script and her heart sank. Up to now she had typed only audio tapes for Canon Wheeler and so had no experience of his handwriting. The only legible thing in it was the peremptory note about when it was required. The other five pages, Julia saw, were all illegible. It appeared to be a sermon, of which, unlike a letter, she could not guess the content. The pages swam before her eyes. Here and there a word emerged; she thought she detected 'the', 'and' and 'hope' through the fog of her panic. Who would know how to decipher Canon Wheeler's execrable hand? She dare not ask Miss Coldharbour. It did not seriously occur to her to approach Canon Wheeler himself. In desperation she thought of Ian and Theodora. Surely they must be familiar with his writing? She took the folder and shot upstairs from her own tiny cell at one end of the double cube. Tentatively she tapped on the door.

'Come in,' said Theodora's firm voice.

Julia slid into the cramped quarters in which Ian and Theodora worked. Ian was not there. Theodora looked up and Julia explained her dilemma.

'It does look a bit like early cuneiform first time round,' said Theodora pleasantly. 'But actually, once you've got the hang of it, it's not too bad. He leaves out the vowels. If you notice, when he speaks he tends to run words together towards the end of sentences and he does the same when he writes.'

Julia had not noticed.

'If you leave it with me for an hour, I'll pencil in the vowels and divide up the words at the end of the sentences.'

A premonitionary reluctance swerved through Julia's overwrought emotions, but she could see no rational reason to refuse.

'Fine, thank you. It shouldn't take more than an hour to type up. May I look in about eleven?'

She clattered back to her office and pounded away at the audio letters for an hour and a half, broken only by a trip to the kitchen for coffee. At a quarter to eleven she galloped back up to the attic room. Neither Theodora nor the script were to be seen. Panic surged through her. Where the hell had Theodora left the script? Where was Theodora? She looked again over Theodora's desk. Absolutely no trace of the script. She ran downstairs. On the landing outside Canon Wheeler's door she came face to face with Miss Coldharbour.

'Canon Wheeler would like to see you in his office at once,' she said distantly. 'Knock once and enter.'

Julia could think of no appropriate reply. In fact, when she came to consider, she never felt that there was any reply that she could make to Miss Coldharbour, whose remarks frequently had the air of concluding conversations rather than opening them.

Julia took two deep breaths, felt infinitely worse and tapped on the mahogany panel of the door. She turned the handle and went in. Canon Wheeler was seated at his enormous desk in front of the ghastly picture of Marsyas. He did not look up as she advanced down the long and beautiful room. She stood in front of his desk.

At exactly the right moment, just when Julia's nervousness had reached its height, he looked up and fixed his prominent grey eyes on her, his handsome regular features flushed with temper.

'Would you kindly explain to me why you have allowed a confidential document belonging to me to fall into the hands of a junior member of my staff?'

He made it sound as though she had given his sermon to the messenger boy.

Julia flushed deeply, 'I'm extremely sorry . . .'

Canon Wheeler had no intention of allowing her to say anything. He simply raised the volume of his voice slightly and continued as though she had not uttered.

'You appear to be ignorant of the proper way to behave in an office of this kind. I do not feel that I should have to instruct even junior typists that my documents, all my documents, are entirely confidential.'

'But,' began Julia incredulously.

'Please do not interrupt me. You will not in future, if you are to remain with us, allow any papers of mine entrusted to you to pass out of your care. Do I make myself clear?'

Julia could trust herself only to nod.

'Would you have the courtesy to answer me?'

'Yes,' said Julia and added, 'Sir.'

* * *

Having disciplined his typist, Canon Wheeler felt much refreshed. He picked up his phone.

'Gerald? I wonder if you'd care to wander up for a few minutes and we could perhaps move this matter of Gray on a bit? Rather than having the police putting their big feet in it all over the place.'

He paused and laughed. 'I had a word with the Chief Constable last night. He's a bit worried about the Old Man.' There was another pause. 'Yes, yes, fine. See you in five minutes then.'

He pushed the appropriate phone buttons and said incisively, 'Rosamund, sherry for three at twelve fifteen sharp, here. And ask the Archdeacon to step up now, would you?'

There was nothing Charles Wheeler liked better than issuing orders. He rightly felt that he did it well. He'd had plenty of experience of orders. His early years had been spent cringing under those of his terrifying and frequently drunken Scottish father. After a rather brutal schooling in Glasgow, he'd moved south with his, by now, widowed mother. Here, little by little, things had changed. The unnatural state of his early years had been reversed. He had managed to haul himself into a position where he gave rather more and received rather fewer orders and proceeded to look around to see how he could get out of the insurance office where economic necessity had landed him and where he had learned only a flashy taste in clothes and stationery. Welcomed in his loneliness into the congregation of a lively evangelical parish church in a northern suburb of London, he had come to see how he might be finally delivered from inconsequence. He immersed himself in parish work and made himself indispensable to the overworked parish priest. The man showed his gratitude by recommending him to the Bishop for ordination. A mature scholarship to Oxford followed, where he acquired more refined snobberies than those afforded by the community of insurance clerks. The not very exacting demands of a theology degree gave him time to make a lot of useful Anglican friends. In fact, he made it a rule never to make any friend who could not be useful to him. He entirely lost his Scottish accent and, after theological college and ordination, preferment had been fast. A minor canonry at a minor cathedral and a chaplaincy to an incompetent bishop had finally produced the reward, at forty-two years of age, of a residential canonry at a respectable cathedral. Canon Wheeler's ambition was a bishopric before he was fifty. He had never heard anyone give more orders than his present Bishop and he dearly wanted to try his hand. The great thing, he decided, was not to get trapped in the *cul de sac* of being a suffragan.

Canon Wheeler allowed his eye to wander around the handsome room lit by the full, secure English sunlight and gazed for a moment through the window at the spire of Medewich's beautiful Cathedral. He was almost tempted to say a prayer of gratitude to the God who had brought him out of Egypt but his contented contemplation was interrupted by the opening of his office door. The soldierly figure, who, confident and elegant in light tweeds, now walked through it was that genuine article for which Canon Wheeler mistakenly thought himself possible to be taken. The Very Reverend Gerald Landsdown, Dean of Medewich, was a member of the cadet branch of the family of the Earl of Medewich and Markham. A competent scholar who had an inbred regard for the pastoral needs of country congregations, he was exactly suited to his place, upon which he never needed to insist, and its responsibilities, which he more than adequately fulfilled. What he thought of Canon Wheeler, if he thought of him at all, he had never, in his gentlemanly fashion, revealed to anyone. Such energy as he had to spare from his clerical duties was expended on the cultivation of orchids for which he enjoyed a national reputation. Today he was wearing a clerical collar, as was, more often than Canon Wheeler, his habit.

'Ah, Gerald, do come in,' said Canon Wheeler with real warmth. He knew how to value the genuine article, none better. The man's cousin sat in the Lords with the Bishop. There could not be more genuine worth in human beings in Canon Wheeler's judgement. Wheeler motioned him to an easy chair and made to put away the handsome leather-bound notebook in which he had been writing. After the Dean, Archdeacon Baggley crept in. Wheeler did not bother to look up.

'How very kind of you to come so promptly,' he said contemptuously, turning to his bookshelves.

The Archdeacon reminded himself that an Archdeacon of ten years' standing was senior to a residentiary Canon of three, but his reminder gave him, not for the first time, no comfort. 'Hello, Gerald,' he said looking for a kind word from someone.

'Morning, Dick,' said the Dean kindly.

Wheeler, who was junior to them both, who had contrived to have the best set of rooms in the office and who had successfully requested both men to wait on him, cleared his throat to announce that he was ready to start the discussion. The Archdeacon stopped talking instantly and the Dean crossed his long legs.

'I thought we might have a word about the Gray affair and try to move things on a little in that area,' said Wheeler. Having coined and rehearsed the right phrases he never saw any reason why he should not use them several times, so he concluded, 'We don't, I take it, want the police putting their big feet in it all over the place.'

'I understand Gray's wife's very cut up about it,' said the Archdeacon and then flushed at his unfortunate choice of words.

Wheeler, who never saw any reason not to punish the Archdeacon said, 'I deprecate your choice of words, Dick.'

The Archdeacon mumbled.

'Of course, this is a truly shocking affair,' Wheeler continued in a tone proper for instructing young ordinands in the correct way to deal with the conventional tragedies of life. He was getting into his stride. 'On the other hand, I think we all know that Gray had a problem.' Wheeler paused meaningfully. 'The question is, should we, for the good of the diocese, for the good indeed of the Church, keep knowledge of that problem out of the hands of the police or, at least, the press?'

'Are we sure,' said the Dean, 'that Gray's problem, if indeed he had one, is connected with his murder?'

'There can be absolutely no doubt of that whatsoever,' said Wheeler. 'I can assure you I have it on the very best authority.'

'Whose?' said the Dean stung, by the emphasis of Wheeler's tone, to testiness.

'That, I very much regret Gerald, I can't reveal even to you.' Wheeler's charming smile took the Dean's intimacy and collusion for granted.

'Do we know where Gray was killed?' interposed the Archdeacon.

Wheeler looked at him pityingly. He always pitied people who had to ask for information. 'The Chief Constable was able to divulge to me that they think Gray was killed last Thursday night. The last time he was seen alive was after Evensong at his church at Markham cum Cumbermound.'

'How long had the head been dead, if you see what I mean?' the Dean inquired.

'Apparently about eighteen hours,' said the Archdeacon unexpectedly. Since the others seemed to expect it, he added, 'Our cleaning lady' — Canon Wheeler winced at the vulgarity — 'Mrs Thrigg, told me. She had it from the police,' he added defensively. Then, since this didn't appear to be enough either he hurried on, 'Her nephew is a police cadet. It's not when I wondered about so much as where?'

‘I thought I had made that clear,’ said Wheeler with no attempt at all to disguise his contempt for the Archdeacon. ‘The police simply do not know.’

The Dean looked thoughtful. ‘I rather gather,’ he said, ‘the police may be looking at Gray’s connection with that man Jefferson. You remember, Dick,’ he turned to the Archdeacon, ‘he knew him when he was a curate at Narborough?’

The Archdeacon nodded. ‘I really can’t see what they hope to find there. Jefferson came to Church youth work with very solid credentials. His regiment’s chaplain spoke of him in the warmest terms as a man of the highest principles. He ran the Narborough club very competently. It’s not an easy patch. Some of the elements are quite tough. I can hardly see him killing Gray. Indeed, I gained the impression he was a firm friend.’

‘I also gather,’ continued the Dean, glancing this time at Wheeler, ‘that Gray may have known that rather odd set-up on the wherry where your man Caretaker lives.’

Wheeler did not care to be connected in any way with anything which was at all unconventional. He felt intuitively that unconventionality was a type of failure, and failure, however distant from himself, might be contagious. He hastened to remove himself from the danger. ‘There may well be something for the police in the Jefferson connection. I really wouldn’t care to speculate. As to Caretaker I think you know my position there. I’m not at all happy with his work. I indicated to the Bishop when I agreed to take the canonry that he didn’t possess the personal qualities I require in my subordinates. I think it may well be necessary for Chapter to terminate his contract with us in the near future.’

‘My own impression of Ian is that he’s outstanding as an administrator,’ said the Archdeacon with real surprise.

‘I’m afraid you’re quite mistaken,’ Wheeler said rapidly, his tone kind and forgiving. The Archdeacon felt baffled. Wheeler’s speech contained so many errors of fact and so many suppositions of value which he did not share, that words failed him.

The Dean interposed. 'You can't sack a man because of his friends,' he said forthrightly, 'and Caretaker's family have been in Medewich a long time. His father knew the Bishop.'

The Archdeacon joined in the defence. 'And I rather thought Ian was a friend of young Thomas, the Bishop's son. They must have been up at Cambridge about the same time. In fact, now I come to think of it, wasn't there some business they were all involved in with young Cumbermound. What's his name, Geoffrey? Not an entirely desirable young man but I'm sure all that's in the past now.'

'Not merely is his work increasingly slovenly but his manners are unsatisfactory,' Wheeler continued as though the Dean and the Archdeacon had not spoken.

The Dean was not prepared to get into a wrangle with Wheeler about a diocesan servant. Nor did he say that he thought it was unlikely, on the whole, that the Bishop would sack a perfectly competent administrator who happened not to be smarmy enough to some thruster from the Scottish lowlands. If it came to unknown backgrounds, after all, no one seemed to know too much about Wheeler's.

'What about Gray's problem, as you call it?' asked the Dean. 'Do the police know about it?'

'Speaking for myself,' said the Archdeacon, 'I very much doubt if Paul had a problem in the sense you mean. You'll remember when we had to look into that last business, Gerald, at Narborough. I formed the opinion that there was absolutely nothing undesirable in the case. Gray had, at the most, been a shade injudicious, a little unworldly, perhaps, in his supervision of Jefferson. As for the police . . .'

Wheeler clicked his tongue, as much in irritation that the conversation should continue so long without his leading it as in deprecation of the mention of police, and past history discreditable to the Church. 'I think you can take it from me,' he said authoritatively, 'that the police are bound to find out about Gray's problem, which, if you'll forgive me Gerald, I fear he really did have.' He smiled companionably at the Dean once more. 'We are all men of the world' — he excluded the

Archdeacon from eye contact and addressed himself exclusively to the Dean — 'so of course we know, do we not, that problems of that sort for young clergy bring with them all kinds of undesirable connections. I'm sure that it's there that the police will be best advised to make their inquiries. I hope you will agree with me, therefore, that it would be in all our best interests to let the police into our confidence on this one. I'm sure you feel as I do that openness is the best policy in these affairs. If you like I could have a word with the Chief Constable and put him in the picture, should you deem it appropriate.'

Let him get on with it, thought the Dean who knew the Chief Constable well. He noticed too that, in the space of twenty minutes, Wheeler seemed to have changed his tack entirely about informing the police.

'That's awfully kind of you, Charles,' said the Archdeacon conciliatorily.

'However,' said Canon Wheeler clearing his throat to indicate that he hadn't finished and intended to keep the reins of conversation in his own hands, 'what chiefly worries me at the moment is the Old Man's reaction.'

Both the Dean and Archdeacon gazed stonily at their boots.

'You do realise that the Bishop is not at all well?'

Clearly they both did and equally clearly they weren't going to help Wheeler out over this one.

'He was kind enough to give me a few minutes after Evensong yesterday.' Wheeler's mandarin-like courtesies when referring to the Bishop reached the point of parody. But no parody was intended: when he got his bishopric, he would expect and require his subordinates to refer to him with similar flourishes. He was celebrating, as it were, proleptically. 'He more or less said that he'd leave the arrangements for Gray's funeral and requiem in my hands and that, as for the press, Chapter could deal with them as they liked. He didn't seem to grasp that we can hardly bury a head without a body. It would be most indecorous. In fact, I think canon law prevents it. I'll have to look that one up. He really seemed not to be quite on the ball.' Wheeler did not add that for a man whose chief pleasure in the past seemed to have been in giving other people orders, a falling off of that activity boded ill. 'I do think, and I'm sure you share my feelings on this one,' Wheeler continued minatorily, 'that he needs our especial support at this juncture. I also wonder,' he added, in his real anxiety dropping into a more common-place diction, 'what on earth's up with him.'

The Dean, who thought he knew what was wrong with the Bishop, who pitied him and prayed for him daily as a man of his own kind, had absolutely no intention of enlightening Wheeler.

'I think,' said the Archdeacon, 'that since his wife died and his son's—' he hesitated '—death, he has withdrawn too much into his own company. I was wondering if he might not be asked out a bit more. Would he, I wonder, dine with us as he used to do?' He spoke with a gentleness that explained why, as a pastor of the parochial clergy, he was by no means despised, however his colleagues might treat him.

Canon Wheeler was impervious to the gentleness but grasped the opportunity. His own preferment was not a little due to his discerning hospitality. If there was anything to be done in that line, he would do it and do it excellently. He glowed now at the Archdeacon. 'I think that's a splendid idea, Dick.'

The Archdeacon beamed in the unexpected light of the Canon's approval. Wheeler turned to the Dean. 'Would it be appropriate to include one or two old friends of his, do you think? I believe he knows your cousin.'

'George likes him. I expect he'd rally round. Get that splendid girl of yours to give me a date or two and I'll see if we can fix something up fairly promptly.'

Wheeler was delighted. The prospect of his giving a dinner party for the Bishop of Medewich and the Earl of Medewich and Markham afforded him a very straightforward pleasure. It was five past twelve. He got up and reached for the phone.

'Rosamund, I thought I ordered sherry. Would you bring it in at once? And bring my diary with you.'

When Canon Wheeler had finished with her, Julia had wanted to go away somewhere private and weep. This, she determined, she would not do. The thought of Miss Coldharbour's cool glance sweeping her face to detect any sign of tears aided her self-control. She clamped her jaws together and made her way back to her desk. The offending sermon lay on top of her in-tray. With loathing she began to read it through. As a result of Theodora's attentions she was now able to decipher it more or less. The first sentence ran, 'The greatest of these is charity.' With immense reluctance she began typing the copy. An hour and a half later, her script checked, she placed it in Miss Coldharbour's in-tray and started down the stairs towards a late lunch. She met Theodora coming up. The latter glanced at her keenly.

'Are you all right?'

'Yes,' said Julia bleakly. Theodora continued to regard her kindly.

'You look a bit strained.' In the face of kindness, Julia broke.

'I had rather a rough passage with Canon Wheeler over the sermon,' she said, and explained.

Theodora listened intently. 'How frightfully interesting,' she said when Julia had finished. 'I've noticed Charles making that sort of move before. He invents rules which you then find you've broken unaware. There's usually just enough rightness about them to make you feel guilty but not quite enough to stop one feeling resentful and baffled as well. The snake in the grass here is, of course, Miss Coldharbour. I had to go out so I gave your script to her to give. to you. She must have given it straight to Charles.'

Julia gulped. 'Why?'

Theodora reflected. 'I think she acts as a sort of procureuse for Charles. Her husband died about five years ago and she's put all her emotional energy into her job. She's totally loyal to Charles, absolutely discreet and sees it as part of her duty to provide Charles with those emotional satisfactions which set him up.'

'Like bullying women,' said Julia with resentment.

'Yes, and men too. To do him justice he's not choosy. He has a go at Ian every now and then.'

'How does Ian cope?' asked Julia with genuine curiosity.

'To tell you the truth, he doesn't do too well. Ian has a violent streak. I think his natural instinct might be to hit Charles rather hard. However, he hasn't done so yet.'

'How about you?'

'Me?' Theodora seemed genuinely surprised. 'Oh, I think when Charles starts on me, I lapse into a sort of prayer. I feel so sorry for him. It seems to work.' She sounded almost apologetic.

'Well,' said Julia with feeling, 'if he goes on like this, I should think someone will break his neck.'

* * *

Theodora wheeled her bicycle over the cobbles of the marketplace and mounted when they ended. The machine, an extremely strong 1965 upright green-painted Raleigh with a heavy steel frame, had three gears and a sensible large carrier basket at the rear. Beautifully maintained, it had seen her through Cheltenham, Oxford, Nairobi and three years in a large parish in south London. She had seen no reason to abandon it when she came to Medewich two years ago, even though she might now have been able to afford a car.

She left the west front of the Cathedral behind her and turned up Market Street. Having negotiated the traffic bridge, she turned left again on the other side of the river to wobble along the towpath. She passed beside the *Amy Roy* but there was no sign of life on board and she pressed on. The Dutch yacht which had been away last week was back in its mooring beside the wherry, she noticed. She left the towpath where it bore left round the sweep of the river which looked across to the Cathedral's east end and peddled along the road. It wove its way through the commercial dockside industry of the town which gave place, in time, to acres given over to the cultivation of the motor car in all its stages, new, second-hand, and crushed to scrap. She cruised through the 1930s' red brick semis and the 1950s' concrete estates on the east of the town. Soon the traffic began to thin and the road became a long straight fenland route with occasional trees and sporadic bungalows slipping into the dykes. The immense sky opened before her and the warm sun lifted her spirit.

The village of Markham cum Cumbermound had grown on one of the rare patches of clay with which the fens were dotted. Its existence was indicated by a thick belt of trees, beech and oak as well as willow, where the clay gradually reared itself out of the silt. The road began to wind rather than run straight between the dykes. Houses built of brick and flint, of indeterminate age but generally not of this century started to appear. Rounding the corner caused by one of these buildings, Theodora saw the square flint tower with a copula, which announced the presence of the church and village. The vicarage lay to the north of the church adjoining the graveyard; the original eighteenth-century vicarage had been modernised, Theodora noticed regretfully, by the addition of two large bay windows on the ground floor either side of the front door.

She debated whether she would do the church first or the vicarage. Deciding business before pleasure, she dismounted and walked up the front drive of the vicarage. The gravel sweep had more sand than gravel on it and the places which vehicles did not pass over were weedy. The lawn needed cutting and had daisies on it, as well as the remains of a child's tennis set. Theodora's heart sank. If there was one thing she did not care for it was children. She'd forgotten Gray had some. How many, she wondered despondently, and how young?

The original Georgian door had been modified with an Edwardian glass porch. Theodora was faced with the usual dilemma of such contrivances, did one hammer on the outer door (there seemed to be no bell) and risk not being heard or did one penetrate to the inner door proper and risk being judged intrusive? She was saved from that particular choice by a boy of about seven, who had apparently been playing with his train set in the porch. At her approach he rose composedly and, with all the aplomb of someone trained from birth to deal with parish callers, said, 'You'll want to see mama. Wait here please. I'll find her for you.'

Mrs Gray was a tall, fairish woman with a slight stoop or at least a tendency for her shoulders to bow forward round her chest. Her hair was coiled without conviction in the nape of her neck. Her dark grey eyes in her pale face had the look of one who had been crying fairly often and recently. Two deep lines down her forehead and the complete absence of make-up made her look older than her probable forty odd years. It was almost possible to smell the misery and tension in her. Her voice, when it came, was high and strained.

'Do come through to the kitchen, won't you? We're in a bit of a muddle at the moment.' The phrase, which was one she must have used a hundred times to visiting parishioners in ordinary times, took on a poignant inadequacy in the context of the murder of her husband.

Theodora followed the hair-cord runner down the middle of the dark hall to a door behind the staircase which led through to the kitchen. The room was light and whitewashed, with an Aga range, stone sink and red tiled floor. These were not the trappings of some Victorianising interior decorator. They were the original fittings left over from the beginning of the century which the Diocesan Parsonage Committee had yet to get around to modernising. The room smelt of bleach and drying washing.

On the high mantel shelf above what had once been the fireplace was a black and white photograph of a young man's head. Theodora, who had met Gray only once, was surprised by how familiar the rather pretty features were to her. The long straight nose, thin lips and diffident, questioning expression of the eyes set rather close together would have looked as well on a girl.

When Mrs Gray had produced two very passable cups of coffee, they seated themselves at the long deal kitchen table.

'I'm sorry,' said Theodora, 'to intrude on you. I've come to see if I may be of use.' It was inevitable that she should start like that but it didn't save her from a sense of her inadequacy.

'We've had a fair number much less welcome than you,' said Mrs Gray, unexpectedly smiling. 'Most came out of,' she paused to select her word, 'nasty curiosity. The press are unbelievable.'

Theodora realised that, in spite of the woman's appearance and the makeshift air of the house, there was strength and intelligence there. 'How do you cope with them?' Theodora inquired, following her pastoral instincts.

'The phone's been disconnected and there were, in fact, police on the gate the last couple of days. I think they've gone now.' Her voice trailed off.

'How do the children manage?'

The tears which had not been far away came to the surface. 'It's far worse for them. At least Paul's young enough not to realise quite. But Tim, my eldest, feels it dreadfully. He shows it by being angry and rude all the time to everyone. The reporters keep on ferreting around. All they seem to want to do is to dig up bits about Paul's past. And, you know, there isn't any past, not really, not of the sort they want.' She paused.

Theodora said nothing. The need to talk prevailed with Mrs Gray.

'You know Paul had a problem.' Theodora said nothing again.

'I hate,' Mrs Gray burst out passionately, 'people looking for a certain sort of reaction from me about it. I know Paul had problems but I didn't, don't, care. I loved him. I knew about it when we married. He hid nothing from me. He was the most truthful, the most honourable of men.' She was weeping now in earnest. When she'd recovered, she went on. 'I know he wasn't too popular with everyone in the parish. In some ways he was rather young and a bit hasty. There are a lot of old people in the parish.' She paused again. 'He loved the children, you know, although of course Tim wasn't his. I'd been widowed a year when we met. But he gave me Paul.'

There was another pause then Theodora prompted her. 'Have things got worse recently?'

Mrs Gray ran her thumbnail along the grain of the deal table. 'He'd started going into Medewich on Thursday evenings after the Youth Club here. He said he had to drop Mr Jefferson back. Mr Jefferson lived in Medewich. Well, of course, I understand that.' Mrs Gray sounded as though she were trying to be fair. Then she continued, 'He started staying later and later. I suppose he was at Jefferson's. I think he got drawn in.' She said vehemently, 'I hate Jefferson.' After a moment she went on, 'I think he thought there might be some possibility of outreach, of bringing young people into the Church. But I don't know. I don't think it's terribly likely. Do you?'

'Perhaps he felt he had a chance to help,' Theodora said. 'Many of us want to do that.' — But privately she wondered what had really prompted Paul Gray. A wish to redeem an equivocal past by mission? Curiosity? Self-testing? Playing with fire to show that he could? Or was there some other fascination? Why had he returned to a milieu which he must have known was a dangerous one for him? Lead us not into temptation, thought Theodora unhappily. 'Do you think that's where he went last Thursday? I mean the day he died?' she went on.

'To Jefferson's? I suppose he might have done. He just went off after Evensong. I thought he might be going to Canon Wheeler's.'

Theodora was surprised, although she did not show it.

'After his . . . after the business at Narborough, he had to see Canon Wheeler every now and again. I think the idea was that a senior clergy should keep an eye on him, help him and so on. Isn't Canon Wheeler in charge of post-ordination training?'

'Yes,' said Theodora, her tone conveying no more than that this was a fact. 'What makes you think it was Canon Wheeler who wanted to see him?'

'He got a note that morning with the Cathedral arms on it. I somehow supposed it was.'

'But he didn't say it was Canon Wheeler he was going to?'

'No, he didn't say anything. He just burnt it.'

'Burnt it?' said Theodora, and this time she made no attempt to disguise her surprise.

'Yes. He brought it into the kitchen and put it in the Aga. We keep it going through the summer for the hot water.' She indicated the washing strewn around the kitchen.

'Did he usually burn his letters?'

'No. He was rather an untidy man really. But he was angry and I think it was a sort of gesture.' She paused. 'I suppose that's one reason why I thought the letter might be from Canon Wheeler.'

'Did you tell the police all this?'

Mrs Gray shook her head. 'I didn't want to say anything I wasn't absolutely certain about. And I didn't know whether the letter was from Canon Wheeler or whether it had anything to do with his going to Medewich. If he did go to Medewich on Thursday. After all, they still haven't found the car, let alone his body. He might have gone anywhere.'

Theodora considered this. She wondered if Mrs Gray wanted to be fair to her husband and to avoid mentioning him in a role which showed him having to report to HQ, as it were; or whether she wanted to be fair to Canon Wheeler, about whom, her tone suggested, she might share her husband's opinion. Either way, Theodora thought, how like the clergy it was to want to keep the clerical club intact and not let in outsiders. For a moment she almost pitied the police, who would not find it easy to get a straight tale from any of its members. 'Why do you think Paul was killed?' she asked finally.

Mrs Gray looked away and then up at the portrait on the mantel shelf. 'It could only be a madman, couldn't it? And he wouldn't have a motive, would he? Not a rational one, anyway.' Her tone urged Theodora's agreement, begging for reassurance.

'You may well be right,' Theodora said gently.

Mrs Gray seemed to have come to the end of what she wanted to say. Gentle and brisk by turns, Theodora proceeded to business details about interregnum provisions, PCC meetings and inquest arrangements. Gradually she led the interview to a quietus, a normality of future projects. She had no manipulative intention. She knew, had always known from observing her excellent father in his parish, how to listen and console without colluding, to allow and never invite confidences, to know right from wrong and yet never to judge or reject. As she wheeled her bicycle down the vicarage drive, she had a purely professional sense of having done nothing, but nevertheless of having been of use. Mrs Gray was more relaxed now than when she had received Theodora a couple of hours ago and Theodora gave herself up to the pleasure of walking through the church yard to the church door.

The grass was short without being a lawn and the two yew trees on either side of the door were trimmed and supported. She stepped down through the great door knowing, from long experience of the signs, that she would find a well-kept and tended church. And so it proved. A strong smell of polish of all kinds, furniture, brass and floor, mingling with the scent of sweet peas greeted her. At the far end, in the tiny chancel, the sanctuary light glowed. Theodora made her way up the chancel, genuflected briefly and knelt in the silent pew, praying for 'the soul of thy servant, Paul, his family and all who worship here'.

When she had finished, she allowed her eyes to wander round the area of the altar. The peace of the place was extreme and healing. Suddenly she stopped relaxing and concentrated. She noticed something which at first seemed familiar and natural and then, as its significance dawned on her, sinister. There were two large candles on the altar and the one on the north side was of a slightly different colour to the one on the south. Moreover, at its base, clearly to be seen by the practised eye, were the shield, square cross and crossed swords of St Manicus's Cathedral arms.

CHAPTER FOUR: CATHEDRAL OFFICES

The Cathedral clock struck two and Ian Caretaker shifted in his bunk beneath the for'ard deck. It was frightfully hot. He had a slight headache. The tiny movements of the wherry and the gentle, muted river sounds which came to him through the warm night air gave him no relief. But it was not the warmth of the night which kept him awake, nor the hectic business of the day in the office, where they had had to deal with all the additional pressures which the murder had brought to the diocese.

As he went over the events of last Saturday night once more he recalled the complex thudding of the expertly played drum, and his rush into the derelict asylum out-building. He had told no one where he was going but on the following day, Sunday, in the strong light of noon, he had returned to the out-building and searched it thoroughly. He had found nothing more, except that on the beaten earth of the floor there had been a single dark stain, from what he could not tell. It was, however, the candle which puzzled him most. Half an inch from the bottom of the stem were the shield, square cross and crossed swords of the arms of St Manicus Cathedral.

He was at a loss to understand the significance of this. The Cathedral had its candles made, as many cathedrals did, by Farris of London. The Cathedral arms were placed on the largest candles — not the tapers which the pious burnt in the side chapels but the candles which were placed on the high altar. Somehow one of the St Manicus's altar candles had found its way to an out-building of the asylum and had witnessed there . . . what? Caretaker turned his imagination away. An altar candle would not be an easy thing to steal. Moreover, no theft of that sort had been reported to him, which it certainly would have been; or rather, it would have been reported to Canon Wheeler. Wheeler, however, did not always pass on the relevant information to his assistant. Knowledge is power and withholding it meant that Wheeler could then play a blame game with Ian for his not knowing something which he ought to have known. Had this happened in this case? Had candles from the Cathedral gone missing? Had Canon Wheeler not known, or had he known and not passed on the information? And if the latter, was it a blame game that he was playing or some other sort of game?

How, Ian wondered, would he discover which was true? If it meant interrogating Wheeler, he knew he could not do it. Wheeler's manner to him was studiedly insulting. After one or two early passages of arms, when Wheeler had first come into the post, in which it became apparent that Wheeler was prepared to be a good deal nastier to Ian than Ian was to him, Ian had settled for a civil service manner in which he made no attempt to contribute to the department's thinking. In time it had become apparent that, although Wheeler enjoyed giving orders and making speeches, there was not much else he could do. There was nothing between rhetoric and imperative. He had no policies. He lived from hand to mouth making instant resolves every time he opened his mail. The amassing of information, reflection, discussion and analysis which form the necessary seedbed of policy, were outside Wheeler's purview. He lived entirely by impulse. Ian pulled himself up short. His contempt for Wheeler, he feared, was becoming obsessive. Yet he hated to think of Wheeler, who represented everything bogus and hollow, desecrating his beloved church.

Ian shook himself free from his bunk, pulled on his flannels and swung himself up the companionway and on to the deck. It was pitch-black and still oppressively hot. He noticed that the modern Dutch yacht, their constant neighbour over the past six months was back in her berth next to the wherry. He looked toward the Cathedral across the water. Suddenly he found himself awake and alert. Had he imagined it or had he seen a light flickering in the window of the St Manicus chapel? He looked away and then looked back. Yes, there it was again, undoubtedly a dim glow of light in the two small windows of the oldest part of the Cathedral at two fifteen in the morning. Caretaker reflected: if he got the *Amy Roy's* tender out and rowed across, it would take about fifteen minutes. If he went round by either the footbridge or the traffic bridge it would take him longer since the wherry lay about halfway between the two. He looked again. The light was gone. A shadow appeared at his side; Dhani's neat figure was at his elbow.

'What is it?'

'I think there's someone in the Cathedral.'

'Do you want to go and see?'

'Yes and no.'

'If you want yes,' said Dhani carefully, 'I will accompany you.'

Ian was moved. Dhani really was his strength and stay now, as in time past. Ian watched his breath in the Buddhist manner for a moment or two and then laughed. 'It's all getting too fraught,' he said. 'Let's treat it as a pleasure jaunt.' Dhani smiled.

Ian sculled, Dhani worked the rudder. They worked well together and soon they tied up at the town quay. The town was very quiet and once on land, they broke into a trot. Skirting the end of the market they ran round the lawn between the St Manicus chapel and Canons' Court. Here Ian slowed up. He glanced up at the windows of the three handsome houses. No lights were to be seen in any of them. He cursed himself for not having brought his keys. Dhani pointed to the wooden door in the wall of the St Manicus chapel. It was ajar. Ian moved cautiously into the shadow of the Cathedral and pushed open the small door. It led directly into the chapel. From there it was possible to get into the Cathedral only through a large, very heavy door directly opposite the one they had just come through.

Dhani sniffed the chapel. 'There is no one here,' he whispered. They made their way across to the heavy door and it swung open at their touch. Ian was not sure whether it ought to have been locked or not. On the other side they paused. They were in the south aisle of the Cathedral nave, not too far from the great west door. To their right was the nave altar and behind that was the organ loft separating off the choir, presbytery and apse chapel. The latter was a memorial chapel dedicated to the local territorial unit of the Medewich Light Infantry.

Dhani sniffed again. 'Someone here,' he murmured. 'I'll take the north aisle and you take the south. We'll meet by the high altar.' He had spent five years at an English public school, so the layout of Anglican cathedrals was not unknown to him.

Ian nodded. In spite of his apprehensions, the atmosphere of the Cathedral was so familiar to him, its contents so well loved, that he could not feel frightened in it. The darkness was palpable. He turned to his right and padded softly over the familiar, uneven stone floor. Every few yards he stopped, listened and touched the wall with his right hand just above his head. In this way he knew where he was. For, placed at shoulder height at intervals on the walls of the aisle, were memorial tablets from the late seventeenth to early nineteenth centuries. Ian knew each one intimately. He moved confidently from the two charming putti who supported the tablet to Major the Honourable Clement Braithwaite, fallen at Peshawar in 1840, to that of the religious and virtuous Clarissa, relict of Bertrand Hardy of this county. By the time he reached the distinctive Carolingian script of the seventeenth-century monument to Sir Edward Turner, Bart, with its pleasant tag, *Vivit post funera virtus*, he knew he was in the transept crossing.

Here there was more light. The huge nineteenth-century organ case which divided the nave from the choir reared itself up above him. He could not see Dhani but calculated that he might by now be opposite him in the north transept. He made for the central entrance to the choir under the organ and almost collided with Dhani, who giggled. The red sanctuary lamp glowed ahead of them, to the left of the high altar.

Suddenly there was a loud crash. Dhani and Ian broke into a run, taking the high altar steps three at a time. They circled the altar itself, covered the five yards behind it and skidded to a halt in the entrance to the Medewich Light Infantry memorial chapel in the apse. Nothing was to be seen. There was no sound. Ian was breathing heavily, Dhani less so. There was a patch of light from the lancet window making a pattern on the floor of the chapel. Round the walls were the dim forms of the banners and arms hung up, monuments of the Infantry's past campaigns. Suddenly Dhani darted forward. On the altar there lay a long dark shadow. Caretaker watched, breathless. There was a hissing sound and Dhani drew a long silver shadow out of the black one. He held both of them for a moment before turning to Ian and presenting him with a sword drawn from its scabbard. Ian felt the sword edge. It was extremely sharp. Far sharper than any memorial or dress sword should be.

'The weapon,' he whispered. Dhani nodded.

Then in the distance they heard the sound of a door shutting very quietly. Caretaker replaced the sword on the altar and started out of the chapel. He knew exactly which door that one was. He turned to the right and made for the north choir aisle. The door was closed when he reached it but it was not locked. Dhani and Caretaker came out of the Cathedral, emerging on to gravel and looked right. The stately stone gate piers of the Bishop's Palace confronted them. In the first storey a light showed in what was probably one of the Palace's drawing-rooms or studies.

Caretaker's heart sank. Dhani gestured to the door through which they had just come and said, 'That door then?'

'Yes,' said Ian. 'It's known as the Bishop's door. Only he is supposed to have a key to it.'

* * *

'Let's get this straight,' said Inspector Tallboy without any great hopefulness in his tone. 'You and Mr Tambiah were in the Cathedral at two thirty this morning having' — he glanced at his notes in disbelief — 'rowed across from the wherry, *Amy Roy*?'

'Yes,' said Ian. 'I was . . .'

'One thing at a time, if you please,' said the Inspector. He had the light behind him and a WPC took shorthand just out of range of Ian's sight. 'You have lodgings with Mr Tambiah on that wherry and have had since this time last year?'

'Yes,' said Ian, 'I had to . . .'

'Just a moment, please sir,' said the Inspector. How he hated all this, he thought. Give him a nice straightforward GBH case in the back streets of the Cumbermound development any day rather than these smartarse church intellectuals with their fancy words and their finicky manners and their too high opinions of themselves. Getting one of their own lot decapitated and then losing the body. Ceremonial swords all over the place. The theatricality of the thing offended him. It was all very well for the Super to smile his superior smile and say things like 'Culturally, Tallboy, it lifts it out of the common rut of murders, wouldn't you agree?' As far as he, Tallboy, was concerned, he could have it.

It felt as though the whole local aristocracy was towering over him. The Chief Constable fussed around the Bishop, the press had been shut up, or anyway given a damn sight less than they would have been if it hadn't been a priest's body, or rather, head. Then this morning, there had been a note from the Super saying the Dean had requested that the police officers who were investigating the crime should please remember where they were when going in and out of the Cathedral. The Chapter — whatever that was — were anxious that services should be disrupted as little as possible. What did he expect them to do, for God's sake? Say a prayer every time they searched the Infantry chapel?

'And the reason you made that trip,' continued Inspector Tallboy wearily, 'was because you saw a light in the St Manicus chapel window?'

'Yes,' said Ian. This time he did not try to add anything.

'And was it a bright light, sir?' The Inspector stressed the word 'bright' as though talking to a ten-year-old with limited vocabulary.

Ian thought how he hated all this. Why hadn't Dhani and he just kept quiet. But of course they couldn't have just left a possible murder weapon on the altar with their fingerprints all over it. 'It occurred to me at the time,' said Ian carefully, thinking that two could play at infant teaching, 'that it was candlelight, not, that is to say' — he managed contempt in his tone with no effort at all — 'electric light.'

'I see, sir,' said the Inspector stiffly.

Tallboy had a large lugubrious face, arms too long for the shirtmaker to cope with, and an air of fighting his clothes rather than wearing them. At the moment he seemed to find all of them constricting. The two men were in a diocesan office room, directly under Canon Wheeler's, which was used as a conference room. It had the slightly stale smell of such untended places. A polished mahogany table, big enough to seat twenty people, ran down the middle of it. Painstakingly the Inspector took Ian through his movements of the previous night while Ian set his teeth and said 'yes' at intervals. Finally, the Inspector said, 'And what made you feel that you had the Reverend Gray's murder weapon in your hand when you held the sword?'

That's the only sensible question the fellow has asked and I can't damn well answer it, Ian thought. 'It was much too sharp,' he said after a pause.

'I see, sir,' said the Inspector heavily. 'Nothing else?'

'No,' said Ian. It made a change from saying 'yes'.

After Caretaker had gone the Inspector leaned back in his chair and stretched. The WPC flipped through her shorthand notebook and looked up. 'Think he did it?' she asked.

'I hope so,' said the Inspector vindictively. 'Getting me out of bed at three thirty in the morning.'

* * *

Theodora leaned back in her chair and stretched, the confines of her office dictating that she extended up and not backwards. Julia sat on the desk and swung her legs. It was quarter past eleven in the morning. They were drinking horrible coffee from paper cups in Ian's and Theodora's attic office.

'Ian's been with the Inspector since quarter past ten,' said Julia.

Theodora looked worried. 'I shouldn't really be here. I ought to have gone to Markham cum Cumbermound to see the PCC vice-chairman. But I thought Ian might need a bit of support when he gets out.'

Theodora really does make attempts on the Christian life, Julia thought. 'What do they want to find out?' she asked.

'What we all want to find out I suppose: who killed Paul Gray and was it done with the regimental sword from the Infantry chapel?'

'They had Canon Wheeler for an hour first, I gather,' Julia said with relish. The idea of Wheeler being grilled by the police cheered her enormously. 'Something to do with keys for the Cathedral.'

There was a step outside the door and Ian came in. He looked white and haggard. When he saw Theodora he looked surprised.

'I thought you were going to Markham cum Cumbermound?'

'Yes, I was. I am. One or two things cropped up. Would you care for some coffee?'

'They've got the Dean at the moment and the Archdeacon's next. Then they're going over to the Palace to see the Bishop,' said Julia chattily. 'According to Miss Coldharbour, that is. She, of course has the timetable. Is there anything that woman doesn't know?'

'About Wheeler, not much, I should think,' said Ian. 'She's been with him longer than anyone else on his staff. I can't think why she stays because he's no easier on her than on the rest of us.'

'Perhaps she's his paramour,' said Julia, delighted to have found a use for the word.

'Much joy may she have of him. I'd have thought he might be impotent,' said Ian judiciously.

Theodora clearly thought that discussion of Canon Wheeler's sexual preferences had gone far enough. 'I thought Rosamund seemed rather flustered this morning when I saw her.'

Ian grinned. 'I gather Charles made life uncomfortable for everyone after the police had seen him. They're looking into the matter of keys. I rather think heads will roll. Oh, Heavens, I'm sorry.' He stopped in confusion.

Julia said soothingly, 'Why should Canon Wheeler be expected by the police to know about keys?'

'Well,' Ian said, 'he's supposed to be responsible to the Dean and Chapter for Cathedral security. In reality, of course, the vergers keep the keys and do the locking up. But each member of the Chapter has a set and Wheeler is supposed to check them every now and again. If people are leaving severed heads in fonts and monkeying about with regimental relics after hours they'd need keys and naturally it's awkward for Charles if . . .'

Ian did not complete the sentence. The door of the office was opened abruptly and Canon Wheeler's tall figure stood framed in it. There was an uneasy silence. Theodora rose. Julia slid off the desk. After a moment's hesitation, Ian got up. Having obtained his effect, Wheeler said abruptly, 'Caretaker, I want you downstairs.'

He turned on his heel and Ian followed him out, closing the door. Theodora remained standing, polishing her reading glasses vigorously. Julia dropped into Ian's vacated chair.

'Why does Canon Wheeler hate Ian so much?' she asked Theodora. Theodora looked even more uncomfortable.

'Well,' she said after a moment's pause, 'of course they are doing the same job up to a point and that's never an easy pattern of work. But they are very different in temperament. And Ian's very much better at it than Charles.'

Julia was surprised.

'Ian's very competent as an administrator. He manages the detail which bores Charles. His judgement is more balanced and he's better educated and better informed. He had three years in the Civil Service after Oriental Languages at Cambridge. I gather great things were expected of him. Then, quite suddenly, he had some sort of illness, resigned from the Service and went to Thailand for twelve months. Where, I gather, Dhani put him in a Buddhist monastery and nursed him back to health — he'd known Dhani at school and Cambridge. When he came back, he tried for the Anglican priesthood and was rejected.'

'Why?'

'It's always rather difficult to know quite what they are looking for at ACCM and there are fashions in what is acceptable and what is not. But if he started talking Buddhism at them, they may well have taken fright.'

'So what then?'

'His father had been a solicitor in Medewich before he died and he knew the Bishop, so he came here as an administrator. He's been here ever since. Three years, that is. He came a couple of months before Canon Wheeler. Because he's so able he wasn't expected to stay. He's a bit out of place here. I think the clergy wonder what to do with him at times. In some way they don't quite articulate, they feel that he's what they would call unreliable.'

'Too clever by half,' interposed Julia.

'Well, too imaginative and too sensitive certainly. He can't be guaranteed to take the orthodox Anglican view, is what they mean. They can't predict his opinions on every topic in the way clergy feel comfortable with.'

'All that Buddhism.'

'Precisely. And his Cambridge friends were rather wild. Geoffrey Markham, the youngest Cumbermound boy, was up at the same time and they and the Bishop's son, Thomas, formed something of a set. I'm not sure whether Ian has kept up with Markham — who had something of a dark reputation at one time.'

Julia was picking up enough about English society to realise that all this made Caretaker of more consequence in Medewich than she had thought. Ruefully, the thought of her own connections crossed her mind.

'So, why does Ian hate Canon Wheeler?' she asked experimentally, remembering the occasion on which she had asked Ian that same question.

'Ian is deeply religious and Charles isn't. Ian cares passionately about the Church. He has a vision of it as a vehicle which prepares us for the presence of God.'

'And Canon Wheeler doesn't share that vision?'

'I'm afraid Charles Wheeler's vision of the Church is as a vehicle for his own self-advancement,' said Theodora with unwonted severity.

There was a pause. Rather more interesting, however, to Julia than either Ian's or Canon Wheeler's vision for the Church was the very puzzling question of why, when he invariably summoned his subordinates to come to him by phone, Wheeler had today put himself to the trouble of walking up a back staircase to the servants' quarters? What, she wondered, could have provoked such uncharacteristic behaviour?

* * *

Ian walked quickly across the lawn from the diocesan office towards the Cathedral, weaving in and out the groups of tourists, many of them Dutch, who visited the town in summer. He noticed with irritation the clutter of bicycles and even motorbikes propped near the St Manicus entrance to the Cathedral. The Dean and Chapter had recently forbidden parking there and had won as far as cars were concerned, but the local inhabitants had always parked their bikes there and continued to do so. He skirted the heaps of chippings and barrels of tar left by the workmen repairing the paths.

Considering all the insupportable things which Wheeler had spent twenty minutes saying to him, he felt remarkably calm. If the police made Wheeler feel uncomfortable about who had what keys, Wheeler would simply pass this on with interest to anyone who crossed his path in the near future. When threatened, Wheeler would hit out at anyone in sight. Rosamund Coldharbour had been near tears, he had noticed, as he had gone into Wheeler's room.

What interested Ian now, however, was not his relations with his superior but quite another matter. He made his way quickly to the north transept entrance to the Cathedral. Then, turning aside before he reached the porch, he used his own keys to open a small iron-barred gate leading to a narrow passageway. It had all the signs of being the back-stage entrance to the building. There were a couple of old pails and a rotting mophead and a small washing line with dusters drying on it. Ian pressed on down the passage, down two steps, until he came to the small wooden door in the fabric. He thumped his hand on it twice and, receiving no answer, used his keys and entered. The space before him was formed from two segments of the crypt's arcading — the room had been devised in the nineteenth century for use as an office for the vergers. Two partitions of heavy wooden panelling did not quite reach the arched ceiling and the other two sides of the room were formed by the walls of the crypt itself. There was a sink and a fridge which masqueraded as a safe, on one side of the room and, on the other, presses up to shoulder height. A board for keys hung beside the door, each key labelled with a metal tag. The crypt office was empty. On a large deal table in the middle was a copy of the *Sun* open at page three. Over the back of the chair next to the table were two pairs of vergers' white cotton gloves drying.

Ian scrutinised the key board closely but was suddenly startled by the shrill sound of the telephone ringing. He looked round for the instrument and saw it on top of one of the presses. After a moment's hesitation he picked up the receiver.

'Vergers' Office,' he said. 'Caretaker speaking.'

There was the usual battery of clicks and coughs which signalled that the internal communications system of the Cathedral was girding its loins for action.

'Williams, I'd like two this time, after Evensong.'

'I beg your pardon, sir, Williams is not here at the moment. This is Caretaker speaking, Canon Wheeler's assistant.' Long acquaintance with the clergy had convinced him that priests could not tell one layman from the next if they happened to be on their own administrative staff. It was best to identify oneself in relation to one's clerical superior.

There was silence and then a click and the line went dead. Caretaker put the receiver back and turned to the door. In it stood the small, slight figure of the head verger, his silver hair and babyish complexion at odds with each other, as, indeed, was his black suit of the gentleman's gentleman variety and his rather springy gymnast's step. Caretaker looked at him with distaste.

'Hello, Jimmy,' he said cordially. 'Where've you been hiding?'

'I've just been showing the insurance gentleman where the bells are kept, Mr Caretaker. Can I help you at all? Would you like a cup of tea? I was just going to get myself one.'

His tone was ingratiating which was another reason, apart from his mannikin looks, for Ian's disliking him.

'Love one, if it's not too much trouble.'

'That's all right, Mr Caretaker.' The singsong betrayed the Welsh as did the repetition of Ian's surname.

The verger did not bother to remove the *Sun* with its obnoxious picture but, with a smirk, planted the mug of tea on it. Ian found this offensive but, given the amount and type of information which he wanted from the man, he didn't want to antagonise him.

He smothered his dislike and said in a gossiping tone, 'Actually, I'm rather in need of a bit of specialist help at the moment.' Ian looked at the Welshman, hoping the flattery was going to take. Jimmy gave no sign either way. 'We've found ourselves in a spot of bother with the police over at the office. It's about the number of keys to the Cathedral. I think we've probably been a bit lax about checking them out.'

What on earth made him use this appalling Americanism, he wondered. There was no reason for it, except that when he was talking to Jimmy Williams he regularly felt that Jimmy required his interlocutors to act a part. Quite what part was required, he was by no means sure. Still, having slipped into a B-film cop part, he found it difficult to slough off the role. 'I'd really appreciate your help in locating just who had what keys,' he heard himself say.

'Well, as you know, Mr Caretaker, all the Chapter have keys to all the doors except the Bishop's door.'

'All the Chapter? That means the Bishop as well, of course.'

'Of course, Mr Caretaker and of course the Bishop has a key to his own door.' Williams tittered.

Caretaker couldn't bring himself to collude with the titter. 'The Chapter are two light at the moment. Canon Hardnut died at Easter. Who had his keys?'

'I think they came back here, Mr Caretaker.' Williams vaguely indicated the board of keys by the door. 'Or if they're not there it may be Canon Wheeler has them for safekeeping.'

Ian snapped, 'The key under the tab marked "Hardnut" on your board there does not resemble that hanging under the tab next to it marked "Sylvester".'

The Welshman grasped this point rather too fast. 'I think you'll find, Mr Caretaker, that the key under Canon Hardnut's label is the key to his house, not his cathedral key.

We kept it here for Mrs Thrigg's convenience. She continues to do for the late Canon in a manner of speaking.'

'So where's his Cathedral key?'

'As I say, it went to Canon Wheeler or perhaps it's in his house, amongst his effects.'

'And Canon Sylvester has his sabbatical in Rome at the moment. Are his keys with him or did he hand them in before he went?'

'His cathedral keys are the ones on the board.'

'What about his house keys?'

'I don't know, Mr Caretaker, about Canon Sylvester's house keys, as if his going to Rome makes a difference.'

Caretaker wondered if there was something in the syntax of the Welsh language which made this sort of construction more acceptable in Welsh than it was in English.

'But he left you his Cathedral key?'

'Yes. As you see, Mr Caretaker.'

'And the Bishop's door, do you have a key to that?'

'Oh no, Mr Caretaker. Only the Bishop has a key to his own door.'

'What happens when you lock up? I mean, say the Bishop's door was unlocked when you lock up?'

'As you know, Mr Caretaker, we lock up at seven thirty in summer and,' said Williams insultingly, 'at five thirty in winter. Unless of course there is some evening event. Twice a week, Wednesday and Saturday, there is a celebration of Compline in the choir at eight in the evening. His lordship is very assiduous in attending at that service.' He pronounced 'assiduous' like a Welshman. Ian gritted his bigoted teeth.

'So, what if the Bishop's door is open,' he persisted, 'after locking up time? I mean, don't you have any key to repair the Bishop's omission if he should forget to lock his own door?'

The Welshman smiled his forgiving smile. 'His lordship never forgets,' he asserted.

Ian found Williams's assertion hard to believe but he pushed his chair back, conceding defeat. 'Just one more thing,' he said as he turned toward the door. 'Those altar candles we pay so much for, we seem to be getting through them at a fair old rate. How often do we reorder, do you know?'

'Funny you should mention that, Mr Caretaker. Canon Wheeler was inquiring about them only the other week. Naturally he was very happy when I was able to tell him that I recently came across a couple of cases of them we didn't know we had. Old stock, like, you see. So we don't need to worry yet awhile.'

You horrible little Welshman, Ian thought. And in a vain attempt to make Williams jump he said, 'I rather think we may have to tighten up on one or two things round here.'

'I'm sure the Bishop and Canon Wheeler will be able to satisfy the police,' said Williams suavely.

As he turned down the passageway Ian wondered just how true that would turn out to be. The Cathedral could be got into at any time by the Bishop's door, given how unlikely it was that the Bishop in his currently abstracted state should remember to lock it every time he used it. In addition, there was the set of Hardnut's Cathedral keys which might or might not be with Wheeler. No wonder the police had given Wheeler a roasting about security; it was amazing they had a piece of altar silver to bless themselves with. Then, too, there was the matter of the candles. Without scrutinising the accounts and checking them against stock, Ian could think of no way of discovering whether Williams was telling the truth about the number of candles held by the Cathedral. Somehow he couldn't quite see himself doing this. And if there was a leak of candles, where were they going and for what purpose? The one he and Julia had found at the asylum didn't seem to have too much connection with the one Theodora had mentioned she had come across at St Saviour's.

And finally, thought Ian as he walked up through the Cathedral stairs from the crypt office, what does the Bishop want two of after Evensong and why did he put the phone down on me when he failed to get the odious Williams?

CHAPTER FIVE: CLERICAL HIGH LIFE

The Dean put down the watering can regretfully. He checked the humidifier and took his mittens off before locking the greenhouse door. It was Friday evening and the Cathedral clock had just struck six. As he walked up to the house his black bitch, Polly, joined him from behind the compost heap in which she had been happily rootling the past half-hour. She appeared to have been eating.

'You'll blow up one of these days, you greedy old bitch,' said the Dean affectionately. Polly grinned back confidently at him and thumped her tail.

'No, it would not be supper time yet,' said the Dean firmly. 'Another couple of hours, at least, and it wouldn't do you any harm to wait a bit.'

The back door of the Deanery lay open to the evening sun. 'Georgina,' the Dean shouted as he passed through the hall. 'Any messages?'

It was the perpetual clergy inquiry.

'On the pad,' called a muffled voice from upstairs. 'If you want your dress shirt for this evening, it's in your chest of drawers. If you're not dressing, there's a clean one in the airing cupboard.'

The Dean mounted towards the voice. 'I expect Charles will want us all dressed. He's a dressy fellow himself. He'd feel anything less than full fig would be an insult to the Old Man.'

'Are you going to be all blokes together?' said his wife, emerging on to the landing folding a pair of jodhpurs. The Dean gazed affectionately at her: a tall, handsome woman whose company he'd enjoyed immensely for thirty-five years.

'Charles hasn't published a guest list but since he didn't invite you, I rather think we shall be.'

'Evil gossip and improper reminiscence, doubtless,' said Georgina. She was slightly miffed at not being invited. She liked a party and enjoyed the company of Lord Cumbermound, her cousin by marriage.

'I suppose the whole thing was done in a bit of a hurry. Charles only had the idea on Wednesday. To ask wives as well at such short notice might not have been on. We're supposed to be boosting the Old Man's morale. As you say, all chaps together.'

'Well, give my love to cousin George and say we'll expect to see him at Cumbermound for the show on Sunday. Alison's got a nice fifteen three bay, very smart. She'd like to sell him for Dotty. He'd be well up to her weight.'

'I'll tell him,' said the Dean from the bathroom above the sound of bathwater falling from a great height into the ample Edwardian bathtub.

'And regards or respects or whatever is proper to Bishop Thomas, God bless him, poor fellow,' she added, and meant it.

'I'll tell him,' said the Dean.

* * *

Next door, the Archdeacon's shower was not quite hot enough, but he made the best of it. The day had been warm, and since it wasn't, he decided, an occasion for dressing, he settled for a light linen suit which he'd worn rather a lot ten years ago in New Zealand. It made him look a little as though he were on safari. Before he left he slipped in to see his wife. She was propped up on the sofa near her open window which commanded an excellent view of the whole of Canons' Court. The late evening sun slanted in from the west. The Archdeacon came and sat down beside her and took her hand.

'All right, ducks?'

She smiled at him, reassuring him. 'Right as rain, Dick love.'

'Taken your medders?'

'Taken my medders.'

'Don't mind me going?'

'You go off and swap your gossip,' she said warmly. 'Give my love to Bishop Thomas. And notice what you eat. Charles's cooking is always Cordon Bleu. And take a coat,' she called after him, 'there's going to be rain later.'

'Bye, then.'

'Bye.'

* * *

Next door, in the mirror of the basement cloakroom of Canon Wheeler's house, Julia made the final adjustments to a maid's uniform. She wasn't sure whether she was looking forward to the evening or not. Miss Coldharbour had recruited her at the last moment to help serve supper for Canon Wheeler's guests who included the Bishop and the Earl of Medewich and Markham. Somebody had gone sick. Miss Coldharbour had understood Miss Smith had adequate relevant experience in that area. Julia was amazed at what Miss Coldharbour knew about her. She had, in fact, done a lot of waiting at table, including high table, at Cambridge in her eighteen months there with Michael.

It was one way of getting money. Once she'd got known for being presentable, turning up sober and on time, not leaving early with the spoons and able to tell left hand from right, word got round and she'd been passed from college to college by grateful manciples. She did not dislike the work and some of the conversation had been interesting. She'd particularly enjoyed a bout between Iris Murdoch and Professor Anscombe, she recalled, on the relation of philosophy to religion. One of the few occasions, it appeared, when Dame Iris had met her match.

Well, anyway, thought Julia, she couldn't be worse at waiting than she was at typing, so she'd asked what the rate of pay was. For once Miss Coldharbour had looked uncomfortable and said she'd have to ask Canon Wheeler, from which Julia had inferred that they had hoped to get her for free. The idea that she'd give up a precious Friday evening for the pleasure of obliging Canon Wheeler for his *beaux yeux* was a myth she was happy to dispel. They settled on ten pounds for four hours work, eight to twelve. 'But Canon Wheeler would be obliged if you could attend a little earlier to get a head start,' said Miss Coldharbour. Could she manage seven?

The doorbell pealed and Julia shot upstairs from the basement, flung herself through the green baize door and then walked slowly and decorously across the black and white tiled hall. The actress in her thought this could be fun after all.

Canon Wheeler's was the first and largest of the block of three houses which constituted Canons' Court. Unlike most clergy houses, which had either too little furniture in them for reasons of poverty or too much from the wrong sort of inheritance, Canon Wheeler's had just the right amount in the right places. Much of it, Julia had discovered in her inaugural tour, was what Michael had taught her to call good. That is to say it had been made in England between the years 1700 and 1840. It occurred to her to wonder where the money came from to support the style. He probably, she thought, came from a wealthy family.

Julia fell in behind the butler, a handsome auburn-haired Irishman with hands like a conjuror's, whose knowing dexterity she had admired in the kitchen. What he did during the day she did not know but, he'd told them, it was quite possible to be out four nights a week as a hired butler. And you could see and hear enough during them four nights to live by blackmail the rest of the week, he'd said. Julia appreciated his staginess and felt secure in his obvious competence.

The Earl was first in. He was a small, neat, humorous man.

'Hello, seen you before haven't I?' he said as he handed his coat to McGee.

'I've had that honour, me lord,' murmured the Irishman suavely.

'Ah, well,' his lordship said, 'you haven't shot me in the kneecaps yet.'

'Not yet, me lord.' McGee piloted him upstairs to the drawing room, leaving Julia to cope with the next bell which came immediately.

The Dean smiled at her kindly, 'Hello, Julia isn't it? Doing a bit extra?'

Julia smiled back at him with affection. 'May I take your coat?' She found it difficult to say 'Sir', but her manner was perfectly deferential. As she went to the cloakroom with the Dean's coat McGee returned to field the Archdeacon with whom he appeared to share a joke, something about kneecapping.

Julia was about to descend to the kitchen when the bell pealed again. She calculated. The Bishop. She waited to see if McGee would make it back from the drawing room then, fearful lest he should have to ring a second time, she opened the door.

Her eye lighted first on the Bishop's purple vest, then on his pectoral cross of slim, dull, old silver. His face was in shadow, half turned away from her, looking back towards his Cathedral. His left hand, bent with arthritis, curved over a stick on which he leaned so heavily as to give him the appearance of physical deformity. He turned slowly towards her. His large square face with small prune-coloured eyes scanned her without wavering. 'There'll be rain later,' he said as she stepped back to give him passage. With relief she saw McGee descend to her rescue and she slipped into the background as he deftly took the Bishop's coat.

It had been decided sherry would be handled by McGee, supper by them both, port by McGee and coffee by them both. Julia, therefore, slipped down to the kitchen. It was large, commodious and beautifully fitted out. The two *dégagé* ladies, who traded very successfully under the name 'Plain and Fancy' at the dinner parties of the bourgeoisie of Medewich and the surrounding county, were working with that synchronised proficiency of totally competent professionals. How nice, thought Julia, to be so excellent at something. Loading the tray with avocado mousse she decided she really should make an effort to get herself some skills. She was no good as a typist.

However, she balanced the tray with sufficient expertise and edged up the narrow back stairs to the ground-floor dining room. As Julia began to work the room, she realised that the house had been designed and built for just this sort of occasion: it was planned for servants to run. From everyone's point of view it was a pleasure. There was no need to take food through the hall. The back stairs landed you outside a second, invisible, dining room door in the white-painted wooden panelling. Julia observed the difference between the grand front staircase and the back one, with its mahogany broken banisters and its dangerously warped risers. It was serviceable, however. There would be no smell of food in the hall as the guests descended from the drawing room, just that pleasant potpourri and beeswax smell of a well-maintained household. Julia surveyed the dining room with approval. The table drew the eye like an altar. The silver, Victorian and heavy to the hand, gleamed on the cream linen cloth. The Dean's orchids, sent in earlier in the day, were displayed in the centre.

Sherry took three-quarters of an hour and, as the Cathedral clock was chiming the three-quarter, there came the sound of the drawing room door opening. McGee, who had come downstairs to test the quality of the sherry while Mrs Quickly, the plumper of the two cooks, stood at the back door fervently pulling on a cigarette, leaped to his feet, pulled at his black tie and took the back stairs two at a time. He and Julia were rigidly in place before Canon Wheeler held the door open for the Bishop.

Wheeler, who in the past had been unprepared for much in life, was not leaving placement to chance. The guests were seated strictly in order of precedence. Wheeler himself took the head of the table with the Bishop on his right and the Archdeacon next to him. On Wheeler's left was the Earl and next to him the Dean. Before they sat down there was a moment's pause. McGee, who had clearly been primed, did not move and Julia took her cue from him. The Bishop said grace in a Latin form which Julia thought she recognised from Trinity High Table. Then, like a film which had been frozen and re-started, they went to work.

The conversation was of ailments. Prostates, bypasses, hip replacements and renal surgery swung to and fro across the table. God help us, thought Julia, used, at least in conversation, to the best. Surely they could do better than this? They'd be on to central heating systems next. Then she realised how old they all were — Canon Wheeler was the youngest man at the table.

With the fish, the Archdeacon started on Cathedral heating systems he had known with special reference to the antipodes. But Lord Cumbermound had clearly had enough. He'd come for an evening's entertainment and, though the food was good, he'd reckoned on stronger meat. With the shamelessness of the truly selfish man who has never really had to consider another's feelings he stopped the Archdeacon dead and, taking his fork from his fish, said, 'What about Gray?'

There was a pause. The Archdeacon was not a man of agile mind. His thoughts were still with hot air versus hot water down under.

'What?' he said helplessly.

'Where's the body?' asked his lordship with relish.

'I think we've all been rather turning our minds away from that one,' brayed Canon Wheeler, embarrassedly eyeing the unfortunate arrival of the *boeuf en croûte*. He hoped he was expressing the Bishop's sentiments.

'Pretty poor, losing the body,' pursued the Earl censoriously.

'We didn't lose it,' said his cousin the Dean, with irritation. 'We never had it. I mean . . .' He failed to complete his sentence. Really, George was a tasteless oaf at times. They were here to divert the Old Man from thoughts of death, not to rub his nose in them. Forty years ago he'd have kicked his cousin under the table.

'What you need is a decent pack of hounds,' said Cumbermound undeterred. Julia cleared the fish plates and McGee changed from Chablis to Margaux. 'Probably do better with Beagles than with fox hounds in a small area like this. Fox hounds get all over the place if you're not careful.' Julia thought he made the hounds sound like lice. 'They'd find it for you fast enough,' he went on, either not noticing or not caring about the embarrassment of his host. Julia was unsure whether it was the moment to serve the beef or not but she did so nonetheless. Any unfortunate associations they'd just have to cope with.

The Bishop came to the rescue. 'Would you care to be hunted like game after your death, George?' he remarked dryly.

Delighted to get some response at last, Lord Cumbermound grinned his evil grin. 'Wouldn't mind hunting the brutes who did it,' he said. 'Sacrilege, isn't it? Cutting off a man's head. Used to do it to traitors. Seventh Earl put a foot wrong under Henry the Eighth and ended up that way.'

Julia looked at the present Earl's neatly barbered head and immaculate dress shirt collar with interest.

'How can it be sacrilege, if it was done to traitors? It must have been legal,' said the Archdeacon, who had just caught up with the conversation.

'Sacrilege, then, to leave it in the font in the Cathedral. Wouldn't that be right, eh, Canon?' The Earl turned to his host almost belligerently, almost, indeed, as though he didn't much care for him.

Wheeler's fine face flushed with annoyance and he laughed. His voice was impressive, the accent almost a drawl, 'My own view would be that the notion of sacrilege belongs rather to superstition than religion in our age.'

The Bishop cut him short. Having appointed him, he saw no reason to have to listen to him. 'The head is traditionally the receptacle of a man's spirit. The sacrilege lies in the desire on the part of the murderer to mutilate what we understand to be in some sense the image of God. We cannot doubt the intention of such a one to mock our normal human relationships and diminish the value which we properly accord to each other. It is not magic or superstition which is at the heart of the sacrilege so much as morality.' He stopped and toyed with his glass. It seemed he was more moved than he meant to be.

This just won't do, the Dean thought desperately. They'd have to try much harder than this. He wracked his brain. Nothing came. 'Georgina sends you her love, George,' he remarked in despair. 'She said she hopes to see you at your show on Sunday.'

Lord Cumbermound was quite prepared to be diverted, for a bit anyway, with thoughts of his handsome cousin. 'Jolly good. I rather gather Geoffrey, my youngest, has got a nice mare showing. Not that that means he'll turn up himself. Never know where he is these days. Bringing that boy of yours, are you?' The Dean's youngest son was twenty-two. 'Shocking rider. Rides like a policeman. Four holes too long.'

Wheeler, who did not understand the joke, prudently smiled. The Bishop and the Dean who did, laughed. Julia, who had done a fair amount of riding in Australia, chuckled to herself. She wished instantly that she had not. Wheeler glanced at her. Cumbermound noticed her grin and the flush which succeeded it.

'Ride a bit do you?' he inquired encouragingly.

'A little,' she murmured, passing the broccoli.

'Good for the health and the figure,' said the Earl appreciatively.

'You and Miss Smith can go now, McGee,' said Wheeler curtly, addressing himself only to McGee. 'I'll ring when I want you.'

'Spoiling an old man's pleasure, Canon?' Julia heard Cumbermound say to Wheeler before the door closed behind them. 'Are you by any chance prudish?'

Not so much prudish, thought Julia, as snobbish.

In the kitchen the two cooks were preparing to depart. Once the meat was served, they reckoned the underlings could be trusted to deal with pudding and dessert.

'Sent out of the room were you?' drawled the thinner of the two. Her tone was educated, mocking: she didn't see herself as a servant because she wasn't one. Julia wondered what exactly she herself was.

'It's usually a bad sign,' continued the plump Mrs Quickly as she swung her headscarf over her head. 'With the county, it's usually smut. With the townies, corrupt business or politics.'

'And which of those,' said McGee, who clearly had a relationship with her, 'would you think the Bishop and the Canon and the Dean and the Archdeacon are pleasuring themselves with?'

'It does seem a bit unlikely,' admitted Mrs Quickly. 'However, given Lord Cumbermound, it could well be all three.' She took a fistful of napkins in one hand and a basket of empty baking dishes in the other, allowed McGee to open the back door for her and, with her slim companion, was gone.

* * *

It was another hour before they were called back. The *crème brûlée* was served without mishap. Julia kept her eyes clear of both Lord Cumbermound and Canon Wheeler and, leaving

McGee to clear the table for port and dessert, she went upstairs to the drawing room to remove the sherry glasses and set out coffee. She paused to admire the proportions and appointments of the room. Did fine feathers make fine birds? Smaller than Wheeler's office in St Manicus house, with three windows instead of four, in daylight the room commanded an excellent view of the river and the backs of the other two houses of Canons' Court. With its low ceiling, bookcases at both ends and plain, grey marble chimney piece, the room combined comfort and dignity.

Julia cleared the glasses from round the room and prepared to set out the coffee on the drum table beside the chief armchair. Before she could set out the cups she had to remove a large heavy book — *Crockford* — which occupied the centre of the table. She picked it up, misjudged its weight and it fell to the floor with a thud. Five sheets of paper fanned themselves out round her feet. In nervous haste she was bending to retrieve them when her eye caught the name at the top of the first: P. Gray. She gazed at it for a moment. Then she skimmed the familiar awful writing. Underneath the name was what seemed to be a short biography or *curriculum vitae.* Under that, however, were two headings underlined. One read 'Certainly' and the other 'Probably'. Under the first heading were listed:

1 Knows Sgt Jefferson.
2 Narborough — parent trouble.

Under the second head was listed:

1 Bent.
2 Bishop's favourite.

There was nothing else on that sheet.

Julia gathered up the others. She found she was sweating and her breathing had quickened. She heard the sound of voices coming up the stairs. She had time to do no more than read the names on the other four sheets. Hell, she ought to have been downstairs by now. She didn't want to be caught up here or to have to pass whoever it was on the stairs. She pushed the papers back into the large *Crockford* and looked round the room, realising there ought to be a servants' stair to the first floor continuing the one running from the ground floor to the basement. She strode to the panelling, searched, found and stepped through on to the dilapidated back staircase landing, just as the Bishop and Lord Cumbermound were entering the room. As she began hastily to descend the rickety stairs she heard Lord Cumbermound say, 'You're quite right, Thomas, not to let women into the priesthood. Because' — his speech slurred a fraction — 'I'm going to tell you a story I heard the other day which I couldn't possibly tell you if you had a lady Archdeacon.'

Emerging from the back staircase into the kitchen, Julia found McGee ferrying the remains from the dining room, downing in quick succession the remnants of the Chablis and the dregs of the Margaux.

'Five bottles of each drunk,' he said in admiration. 'And a pretty penny that must have set the good Canon back. Come on now, Miss Julie, sit you down and have a glass. You've been on your feet all evening.'

'So have you,' said Julia as she took the proffered glass. And indeed he had. He'd worked hard, smoothly, with humour and enjoyment, thought Julia with sudden distaste, so that five old men could get drunk with ceremony.

They sat down with a glass each before making the final assault on the stacking of the dishwasher ready for Mrs Thrigg in the morning. Outside Julia could hear the patter of rain drops on the back path. It must have started earlier, she thought, absently recalling the Bishop's first words. Then, through the rain, she heard a scratching sound, followed by a sharp, impatient bark. There was a count of three, then the same bark again, like a bell tolling.

Julia grinned. 'I think the Dean's dog has called to fetch him home.'

She went to the back door and opened it. Sitting outside, difficult to see because she was a black dog, was the Dean's Labrador bitch, water from her dark coat dripping and glittering in the kitchen light. The dog had her head thrown back ready to deliver another bark but when she saw Julia she rolled her navy-blue eye in its white socket and smiled. With a gesture which reminded Julia of someone searching their pockets for change, she picked up the present which she had brought to welcome the Dean. Julia was about to let her in when she saw what she had in her mouth. Her cry brought McGee to her side.

'Oh God,' said Julia, 'Oh God.'

CHAPTER SIX: A DISH OF HERBS

Julia lay on her bed in her attic room. She could see the asylum to the north through her open window. The grey weather of the night before had continued and the rain kept sweeping in through it. Julia would not shut the window but sweated and shivered by turns. She had again refused sedatives from a doctor after endless police questioning in Canon Wheeler's elegant dining room the previous night. The body of Paul Gray had been removed from the Dean's compost heap. The entire area had been roped off and there appeared to be policemen every ten yards. Julia, stunned but dry-eyed, had given her statement to the police. She had been followed by McGee, Lord Cumbermound, the Bishop, the Archdeacon and Wheeler. The Dean had gone last and, she judged, been gone the longest. It was three thirty in the morning before they were all allowed to depart. This time Julia had not refused the lift from the police car. Once home, she was surprised to find she slept soundly but woke about noon with the appearance of fever.

She kept recalling the scene in the kitchen. McGee had summoned the Dean, but it had been Lord Cumbermound who had led the party down the back stairs. Though he had lurched into the kitchen like a drunken huntsman, he had known what to do. With the authority of a man used to calling hounds to heel he'd taken the arm from the dog, wrapped it in a towel and set it on the draining board. Then he'd sent McGee to phone the police and the Dean back upstairs to inform the Bishop, who had not joined the kitchen party. Wheeler was paler, tenser than she had seen him before, his hands trembling. Cumbermound had sent him for brandy and glasses. When these had been procured, the Earl, ignoring Wheeler, had poured out two measures, one enormous one for himself, and a smaller one for Julia. When she had shaken her head, he'd taken her hand firmly in his and said peremptorily, 'Drink it. It's going to be a long session.'

Choking, Julia had obeyed.

She could not stop herself recalling the moment when she had realised what it was the dog had had in its mouth. She wondered if she would ever free herself from the memory. She recalled Ian's advice and whenever the picture came before her eyes, she tried breathing it out. She realised that, as she did this, she was almost groaning with her effort to release the horror locked within her. Gradually, she began to feel calmer. She wondered why Caretaker's advice appeared to work and longed to ask him. As if in answer to her wish she heard a heavy, masculine tread on the uncarpeted stairs outside her door. Slightly taken aback, she called 'Come in' to the rather hesitant knock.

Ian edged into the room as though not quite knowing what to expect. He looked down at her with concern.

'Hello, I'm sorry to intrude. I, that is, we, Theodora and I, wondered how you were.'

Julia smiled with gratitude. 'Much better for seeing you,' she said cordially. 'It was kind of you to come.' She pulled herself into a sitting position.

Ian grinned. 'Theodora really sent me to ask if you would care to come to supper this evening on the wherry with Dhani, if you feel up to it? I think she feels you shouldn't be let too much alone but she can't get away herself. Pressures at the office.'

'She shouldn't be in the office on Saturday.'

'Canon Wheeler required his staff to be in, "in the circumstances", as he put it. Actually he wanted someone to give some orders to and to deal with the press for him. For once he seems to be at a loss for words. I'm playing hooky for an hour.'

Julia found herself suddenly weeping. Kindness always moved her more than anything else. Ian looked unhappy but did not disengage his attention from her.

'Try breathing it out,' he said after a moment.

'Oh, for Christ's sake,' said Julia halfway between exasperation and laughter. However, she ceased to weep. 'Tell me the news,' she said, pulling herself together.

'Well,' said Ian, 'I was rather hoping you might do that for me. Rumour, as you may guess, is rife. It ranges from the Dean's having been arrested for murdering Paul Gray to the Bishop's having hired Lord Cumbermound's Beagles to track down the corpse.'

Julia told him as much as she knew. Hesitantly she mentioned the notes in *Crockford*. She noticed Ian flush as she retailed the little she knew of their contents.

'Was it in Charles's handwriting?'

'Yes. Unusually clear too,' Julia added.

Ian walked to the open window and looked up at the hills, with their barracks, prison and asylum perched aloft. 'Charles's drug,' he said slowly, 'is power. When he's in the presence of political or worldly ecclesiastical power, I've noticed there's an almost physiological reaction in him. He gets physically excited. Ambition oozes from him like sweat. His place obsesses him. And until he gets real power he'll make do with deference — subservience even. And he's willing to punish, if need be, to get it. It begins to look as if his obsession has led him down evil paths.'

Julia took note of Ian's tone as well as his words. He may well be right on the evidence she thought, but he's rather too glad he's got something on Wheeler at last. She felt the strength of Ian's contempt for Wheeler. It was wrapped in theatricality but there was real bitterness beneath. Was it, she wondered, justified? She recalled Theodora's remarks about Ian's not being regarded as 'reliable' by the clergy. She remembered, too, Canon Wheeler's unexpected appearance at Ian's attic office when he had perhaps expected to find it empty. Was that how Wheeler gathered his information for his nasty notes?

'Where do you think he got his information on Paul' — Julia corrected herself — 'Mr Gray from?'

'The cv stuff he could get from *Crockford*. It's a sort of ecclesiastical *Who's Who*.'

'And the other stuff, the "certainly" and "probably"?'

Ian turned to her kindly. 'It doesn't amount to more than gossip, you know. There was some sort of a row in Gray's first curacy at Narborough. He was a curate during an interregnum, so he was left very much to his own devices. He ran a youth club with a man called Jefferson, who had been a regular soldier. He was invalided out and qualified with the local authority as a youth worker. Jefferson approached the parish and, since he came with a reference from his regiment's padre, they were glad to use him. But he had a rather military approach to the work and he did run some rather tough courses for some of the boys, so one of the parents complained. But there was no suggestion that Gray had been involved in anything improper and Jefferson continued to be involved in youth work. People with his sort of skills willing to give a bit of time to the Church are in rather short supply.'

'What would Paul's relations have been with Canon Wheeler?' Julia inquired. She really had very little idea of how the diocesan senior clergy connected with the parish priests. 'Would Canon Wheeler have been Paul's boss?'

Ian snorted. 'In no sense, though some diocesan clergy tend to treat parochial clergy as though they were their inferiors. And many parochial clergy react by resenting and despising the chapter. All authority, both of chapter and parish clergy derives from the bishop. In law and theology the priest in the parish represents the bishop to the people. Priests take an oath of allegiance to the bishop at their induction into their livings and at set times, often on Maundy Thursday, they will renew their vows. I suppose the link between chapter and parish is really administratively through the archdeacon. He's a sort of diocesan works manager responsible to the bishop for the smooth running of the parish priests. The chapter are supposed to run the cathedral not the diocese. Nevertheless, because they are supposed to be men of wide experience and outstanding capability the bishop may from time to time give them particular tasks to do in connection with parish priests. This may have happened with Wheeler and Gray. Wheeler may have been "given a charge" as the phrase goes, by the Bishop to keep an eye on Paul when he went to his new parish at Markham cum Cumbermound.'

'I see,' said Julia not being too sure whether she did or not. 'I wish I'd had time to read what Canon Wheeler had written on Jefferson all the same. The other piece of paper had the name J. Williams on it. Do you know anything about him?'

'Head Verger. Welsh,' said Ian unforgivingly.

'I wonder what he'd written on him.'

'Anything would be possible of that creepy little beggar.'

'What's wrong with him?'

'Frankly,' said Ian reluctantly, 'I have to admit I've never caught him out in anything except, of course, of being Welsh. But I'd believe anything of him.'

Julia laughed. 'You're absolutely irrational. I expect he's a perfectly nice man. You said yourself that figuring on Canon Wheeler's hit list doesn't necessarily mean you've done anything disreputable.'

'Someone killed Paul Gray,' said Ian sombrely. 'And it's beginning to look as though he was killed in the environs of the Cathedral. Putting heads in fonts and corpses in compost heaps suggests a fair amount of familiarity with the building.'

'You mean a verger would have that sort of familiarity?'

'Yes. But of course so would many other people. As well as access. The keys to the Cathedral were widely distributed as far as I can make out.' Then Ian realised that wasn't in fact true. There was only one certain way into the Cathedral and that was by the Bishop's door if the Bishop forgot to lock it after him.

'What on earth could be the reason for Williams killing Paul?'

'Ah, now there you have me. But give me a bit of time and I'm sure I can find some cogent motive to pin on him.'

'And what about G. Markham. I saw his name too. Who's he?'

Ian frowned and turned once more to the window. Finally, with every sign of reluctance, he said, 'He's Lord Cumbermound's youngest son. He's no good. I should have thought it would be the easiest thing in the world to write a file on him. I could do one myself. I don't know how Wheeler knows him except that Charles has a cottage on the Cumbermound estate so perhaps he's come across him that way. Markham's certainly not a churchman, though of course the Cumbermounds are the leading lay family in the county. Presumably you didn't have time to see what Wheeler had got on him — if anything?'

Julia shook her head, and this time she was not smiling. She said, 'What do you suppose Canon Wheeler means to do with all those "probables" and "certains"?'

'I think he already exacts a fair degree of pleasure from simply being able to make people jump whenever he calls them up.'

'Money?'

'Oh, nothing so crude, though Charles certainly knows its value and gets through a fair amount. No. You remember how Rosamund Coldharbour set you up for him in the matter of typing that sermon?' Julia nodded unhappily. 'I think it's psychological satisfactions of that sort which he's after and which Rosamund puts in his path. Just letting people know that, if he chooses, he could make life very uncomfortable for them, so they'd better lick his boots hadn't they?'

'But it's perverted,' Julia protested.

'Only mildly so, in the Church's terms at least.'

Julia contemplated the landscape opened up to her by Ian's remarks. She felt a sort of desolation sweep over her, together with something like pity for Wheeler. She remembered Theodora's remarks to her in a similar vein. 'How appalling,' she murmured.

'Deathly for the victim, certainly,' said Ian with feeling.

'I meant for him, for Wheeler,' said Julia meekly. 'To reduce all human relationships to games for that sort of fulfilment is terrible.'

'Certain professions create the conditions in which seeking those sorts of pleasure is almost legitimate. Teaching is one such, the Church another. Certainly, Charles Wheeler isn't the first priest in the Church to get his kicks like that.'

'Where does Wheeler come from?' said Julia suddenly. 'Why isn't he married? I thought Church of England clergy had to be.'

Ian smiled. 'They don't actually have to marry. Celibacy is perfectly acceptable, although rare. As for his previous career, I don't know any more than is in the book you saw, *Crockford*. I think he's Scottish by extraction, though you'd hardly know it from his accent. I've never heard of a wife mentioned in connection with him. I'm pretty certain he hasn't been married.'

'Or divorced?'

'Highly unlikely. The Bishop takes an old-fashioned high church view on divorced clergy. He won't induct them to a living if he can help it and he certainly wouldn't put a divorced priest into a canonry.'

Julia suddenly found herself near to tears again. She longed to ask him more about Paul Gray but could not quite frame the question she wanted to ask. Instead, she said, 'And the fourth sheet of paper? What's Canon Wheeler got on you?'

'I wonder,' said Ian and laughed so genuinely that Julia was reassured. 'I could always ask Canon Wheeler to hear my confession under the seal,' he said wickedly. 'That'd stymie the bastard.'

* * *

Julia stayed the rest of the day in bed, got up and bathed at six, dressed carefully in a green shirt and black jeans, and then walked slowly down to the town. Her fever appeared to have receded, leaving her feeling light and free. She debated whether to reach the wherry by going through the Cathedral grounds and over the footbridge — the prettier way — or whether to use over the traffic bridge in front of the market square. Finding she could not bear to face the police who might still be in the environs of Canons' Court, she decided on the traffic bridge. She bought wine at the off licence on the corner of Market Street and plunged between the bridge's traffic, locked solid on a Saturday evening. With relief, she turned left down the towpath towards the *Amy Roy*. The rain had ceased and behind the wherry's mast was a splendid yellow and grey sky. The Dutch motor yacht had gone again, leaving the *Amy Roy* to form a nineteenth-century watercolour on her own.

Julia climbed on board without hesitation, sure of her welcome, relieved and delighted to be with people whom she trusted. She made her way aft to the companionway and, hesitating a moment, called, 'Hello.'

Dhani's not quite English voice answered her. 'Down here. Come down.'

She descended the steep mahogany steps into the galley, beyond which lay the living space in the converted hold. Dhani smiled at her and his whole face illuminated when he did so.

'You're most welcome,' he said. 'You're the first. How are you feeling after your ordeal?'

'Fairly recovered, thanks,' she assured him.

He regarded her. 'It will leave its mark, I think. Are you dealing with it?'

'Ian keeps telling me to breathe it out,' said Julia half smiling.

'Sound advice,' said Dhani. 'You must not suppress it. You must allow all the horror of the picture to visit you as often as it will. Do not thrust it aside. On the other hand, do not dramatize or exaggerate it. Just let it stay with you and then breathe it away.'

He knows. Julia thought. He's experienced horrors and he's dealt successfully with them. He spoke with authority and she trusted him. She could see why Ian did too.

She came further into the kitchen. 'Can I do anything to help,' she asked.

'Yes,' he said. 'Chop some bread up, could you, and take it through? They won't be long now, I think. Thank you for the wine.'

While she was chopping she said, 'You've known Ian a long time?'

'I came into the first form of his boarding school. He was extremely kind to me. If he hadn't been, I should have made many more mistakes than I did and been more unhappy than I was. He had, in some respects, a maturity beyond his years. Later, I returned to Thailand and he came out and stayed with us. He enjoyed it, I think. He liked my mother; he lost his many years ago. We are rich — diplomats. It was Ian who persuaded my father to let me go on to Cambridge, which I did a year after Ian. Do you know Cambridge at all?'

Julia considered. 'In one respect, yes, I know it. I lived there for eighteen months with someone I thought I loved, indeed who I did, do, no, did love.'

Dhani looked at her quizzically, 'It doesn't die, does it? Only changes.'

'In my case,' said Julia thoughtfully, 'it changed to hate.'

'That's bad,' said Dhani.

'Yes, it is. I can see it is. But I can't quite see how to deal with it yet. And don't tell me to breathe it out. I haven't finished with it.'

Dhani smiled, 'I wasn't going to suggest anything so radical. As you say, you are clearly not yet ready for that solution.'

'Dhani, why does breathing it out work?'

'Don't you say in one of your Christian writings, "The Lord is the breath of life"?'

'I don't know,' said Julia. 'I'm not a Christian and I'm not educated.'

'If you are Western European by descent then you are Christian,' said Dhani authoritatively. 'And you appear to underestimate the degree of your education, if I may say so.'

'But Christianity doesn't mean anything to me. It just seems to be a sort of club for the clergy.'

'You speak of Anglicanism, perhaps, not Christianity.'

'I suppose so. But even as a club, Anglicanism doesn't seem to be terribly—' she hesitated, 'effective. I mean they can't even be kind to each other let alone other people.'

'What about Theodora and Ian?'

'They aren't clergy.'

'Theodora is, I think. And I'm sure she would say that Anglicanism isn't just the clergy.'

'Well,' said Julia, 'she's different. And yes, I think that what the clergy are, Anglicanism is. They seem to set the tone.'

'What about the Dean, of whom I have heard both Theodora and Ian speak with affection?'

'Well, yes. But in some respects he seems to be left over from a previous age. I feel when he's gone they won't be able to replace him. Canon Wheeler is the modern type.'

'That one sounds to me like an archetypal priest,' said Dhani. 'There's nothing new about proud prelates with suspect backgrounds.'

There was the sound of confident feet descending the companionway and Theodora entered the galley. She had brought an offering of apples and bananas. 'Good evening, Dhani. Good evening, Julia. How are you after your ordeal?'

'Theodora,' said Julia bravely, 'is breathing it out in Dhani's system the same as praying in yours?'

'Yes,' said Theodora finding no difficulty at all in launching straight into theological discussion while arranging her fruit in a bowl. 'There are, of course, certain differences in credal formulation between the two traditions. I mean, the way in which Christians and Buddhists would describe what they do in terms of their own systems might differ. But at the level of experience, essentially the foothills of prayer are a matter of modifying our consciousness in certain ways and breathing is a way of purifying the affections. "Make clean our hearts within us", you remember.'

Julia didn't but didn't like to say so. 'Do you think you can do it with drugs?' she asked.

'No,' said Theodora and Dhani together.

'Always refuse sedatives,' added Dhani. Julia smiled.

They moved from the galley to the main living area of the wherry. This had clearly been modernised. Bunks ran down the side and a cabin table marched down its centre. The ceiling, which was, of course, the deck, was so low that Theodora had to stoop. The whole area smelt of polish and resin. The light supplementing that from the small portholes came from a central paraffin lantern. In the middle of the table was an earthenware bowl of cow parsley and larkspur.

There was a second clattering of footsteps and Ian appeared, his tall figure framed in the sliding door. The smell accompanying him suggested he'd brought fresh coffee beans. Dhani took them from him, smiling.

They ate the *hors d'oeuvres* of eggs and mushrooms, then a vegetable stew of beans and aubergines, onions and tomatoes with a green salad. They finished with a dessert of nuts, honey and apple. Theodora, Ian and Julia drank the white wine followed by coffee. Dhani drank water followed by herb tea. There had been no grace but before they ate Julia noticed a moment's silence had descended. It was certainly as ceremonious in its way as Canon Wheeler's dinner party the previous night but no one was drunk, no one on edge, no one competed with another. The reined-in impatience which so often emanated from Ian was absent, Theodora's gravitas was mitigated and Julia's social nervousness sedated. Dhani presided and served at the same time. Julia compared the food of the two parties and decided unhappily that she liked both the dish-of-herbs meal of this evening and also the elaborate deliciousness of avocado mousse, sole and *boeuf en croûte* of the previous day. There's no hope for me, she thought. She lacked discrimination.

About the company, however, Julia was in no doubt as to her preference. They were, she realised, respectful to each other and kind, as to valued equals. Their backgrounds were diverse but their perspectives similar. There were no servants.

When they had finished eating, Dhani turned to Theodora and, as though commencing a liturgy, inquired, 'Has the moment come?'

Julia was aware of something which had been planned beforehand yet it did not discomfort her. The quietness of the long cabin room, the dim lighting and the remains of the shared supper, all contributed to the feeling of a ritual being celebrated. Theodora glanced round at Ian and Julia and answered composedly, 'Yes. I think the moment has indeed come.' She focused her gaze on Julia. 'I feel we should try to talk about the happenings of the last few days. There are forces loose here, types of evil, which are corrupting our energies. These are outside us but also within us. We need to bring them into the light and recognise them so that we may dispatch them.'

Julia nodded, slightly bemused, yet accepting. Theodora turned to Dhani, who replied, 'We need therefore to talk truthfully about what we feel as well as what we have witnessed. That is always the first step.'

Theodora then looked at Ian. He, in turn, picked up the theme. 'We can't replicate the police investigation and solve Paul Gray's murder. But I'm sure there's a landscape of emotions which forms the background to murder which is quite as important as the foreground of material events.'

Julia's heart was suddenly moved within her. What these people have in common, she thought, is the ability to use words like 'truth' and 'evil' without embarrassment or meretriciousness. They were completely serious moral beings living in a world where such terms usually had no content. They could have told you what they meant by them and they gave them a currency in terms of their own conduct. They weren't out to impress or wield power. They weren't like anyone that Julia had ever met before. The casual or predatory affections and competitive ambition which had characterised her acquaintances at Cambridge were of another and lesser world. If anyone could help her, Julia thought, these could.

'Julia,' Theodora said, 'since the affair began with you, would you like to lead off? It does not matter that we already know to some extent what has happened to you. Tell us again in the words you choose. Nothing,' she added reassuringly, 'nothing is irrelevant. Nothing will bore us. Fear not.' She smiled. 'Breathe it out on to us.'

Julia was silent for a moment. There were things she had not told them. Yet she had not been required to tell them: they had not asked. Now she was clearly being given the opportunity. 'I wonder if I might begin with my family,' she said. 'It would give me some sort of starting point.'

Dhani nodded at her. She continued.

'My father was an English chemist. Through his work he came to Australia, where he married my mother, an Australian. I was born in England and lived here until I was seven, then we returned to Australia. I don't think my parents were entirely happy together. My father was killed in a car crash when I was twelve. My mother, out of guilt, perhaps, became addicted to tranquillisers and drink. She was dead within five years. I had a little money from my father's will, administered by his British solicitors. I came to my father's cousins in England and went to live in Wolverhampton. While I was at the local Further Education College I met Michael. I'd never met anyone so ambitious and as single-minded. He wanted to do Natural Sciences at Cambridge, worked terribly hard and got in. He invited me to go and live with him and I did. We were happy for about nine months and miserable for another six. I watched him growing out of me. I didn't have his scientific interests. I had no foundation of my own from which to develop. I could do him no good. I couldn't further his career in any way or extend his mind. I seemed to have no value for him and it began to feel like a kind of death. We ended up hating each other. In desperation I took a typing course and moved fifty miles down the road to here, to the first job which would have me. What I mean is,' Julia stumbled, 'perhaps my inglorious life story isn't relevant to what we're supposed to be doing here. But I, too, feel without place — so I can identify with Paul Gray. I know he didn't fit into his parish as well as he would have liked. I don't fit in anywhere either. I feel as much a severed head as he is. I'd like . . . I'd like his murderers found. I want to know why they did it and especially why they did what they did with the head . . . It's not exactly revenge I want, but I'd like things evened up. A balance restored.'

Julia stopped and then added in a quick toneless voice, 'The actual facts you already know. On the day of my interview for that job, I found a woman, Mrs Thrigg, in hysterics in the St Manicus chapel, beside the font. In the font she had found the head of the priest.' She paused, drew breath and battled on. 'A week later, while employed as a servant to Canon Wheeler, I . . . the dog . . . my . . . the arm of the corpse of Paul, of the priest, was brought into Canon Wheeler's kitchen by the black dog.' This time she stopped in earnest. She realised what a relief it was to have formulated that simple statement and how, having done so, the power of it to horrify her was already lessening. 'That's all,' she concluded.

Theodora said gently after a pause, 'Have you told us everything?'

'No,' said Julia, 'I haven't.'

Theodora prompted her, 'The priest.'

'Yes,' said Julia after a moment. 'The reason I chose to come here for a job was because I thought I had relations here. Paul Gray was a second cousin.'

Theodora murmured, 'I'm so very sorry. How appalling for you. When did you first realise?'

'When I first saw the head in the font it just looked familiar — I couldn't sort out why. Then I saw the photographs in the newspapers, and I was still unsure. I last saw my cousin when I was seven and he was seventeen. But his looks were distinctive and very much of my father's family. He was red haired, grey eyed, thin faced. I thought him very handsome when I was seven. He was also kind, I mean to me, at that age.' Julia bent her head to conceal the tears which she could no longer restrain. 'I sent to my Wolverhampton cousins for confirmation. I know now that it was him.'

There was silence, eventually broken by Caretaker. 'It's the severing of the head and placing it in the font which is so brutal, isn't it? A sportive horror.'

Theodora nodded. 'Would you say, Ian, that the Church could produce someone capable of an act of that kind? Are we to look within the Church for those kind of murderous emotions?'

Ian reflected. 'The Church is certainly capable of hurting people deeply. At times it seems as though it may have been evolved to do just that.' He looked across at Theodora as though seeking permission to continue.

'You spoke of a moral landscape for murder,' she said, 'Could you expand on that for us?'

'The focus of my own emotions,' said Ian, 'is not, as I think Julia's is, my family, whom I have always been fortunate enough to be able to take for granted, but rather it is the Church, about which I'm unduly passionate. While I was at Cambridge, I began to follow a rule of life which I hoped would prepare me for the priesthood. When, later, I joined the Civil Service, I found it hard to follow that rule since I was constantly required to lie. I resigned and went to stay with Dhani's family in Thailand. While I was there, I went for a time to a *sangha*, a Buddhist religious community. It would have been very easy for me to stay there for the rest of my life. Their rule is perfect and effective at the practical level, but I could see no way of passing its benefits on, of helping or involving others. I wanted salvation, you see, for all. It will be apparent to you that I have, in my way, the largest ambitions. Almost indeed, Messianic ones.'

Theodora nodded. This was entirely typical of Ian, she felt. From these huge ambitions came both his weaknesses and his strengths. The clergy sensed it too, she suspected and, feeling the lack of a matching religious passion in themselves, edged nervously away from him. 'When I returned to England,' he continued, 'I asked Bishop Thomas to recommend me for ordination to the priesthood. He had known my father for many years. He said that he would. I was not, however, accepted by the Board of Ministry. Instead I came to work as a layman at the diocesan office.'

Ian stopped, and Theodora said gently, 'I know you're passionate about the Church, Ian, and I know you were deeply hurt by its rejection of you. But are there things nearer home, in our own diocese, which might help us to understand the murder of a priest?'

Ian resumed. 'When I had been here about six months, I became aware of certain tensions both in the diocese and amongst the Cathedral clergy, the Chapter. It was not just the usual enmities and silly Trollopian rivalries of a narrow society living very much in each other's pockets. Nor was it the traditional and risible gaps between the spiritual duties of the clergy and their worldly preoccupations. It seemed to me that there was some quite palpable fear, some terror, almost, loose amongst them.'

'Whom is that terror affecting, do you think?' Theodora asked quietly.

'The Archdeacon is unreasonably frightened much of the time. I think, too, that Charles Wheeler's bullying arrogance is a defence against some fear that he cannot face. But most of all I am aware of it in connection with the Bishop. It's not just that he has withdrawn from the business of running a diocese, or that he walks abroad a great deal at night but is scarcely seen during the day, or that he often won't accept phone calls. It is much more that he seems to be playing games. He sets the clergy against each other in rivalry for his favours. He selects "sons" — Gray was one such — and seems to seek the psychological satisfactions of their gratitude and deference. Whether this fits into the pattern of circumstances which brought about Gray's death, I don't know.'

'I've wondered about the implications of the placing of the head in the font,' Theodora said thoughtfully, 'and what you say about the possibility of its being a symbolic gesture. It mocks by its obscenity. I wonder whether whoever did it was making a gesture in the direction of the Bishop, as if to say "This is your beloved son".'

'There is one further matter,' Ian went on. 'Each year, I have to prepare the accounts of our department's affairs for the Diocesan Secretary. For the past two years I've felt that there was something odd in some of the accounts. This year I'm nearly certain that there's been some money, not too much — about five thousand pounds — taken out of the system. I haven't mentioned this to anyone and I'm not sure whether I've got enough evidence to make a case yet. But my feeling is that someone has had their hands in the till. Again, I don't know if this has any bearing on the murder of Paul Gray, but it does seem to me to be a part of the general atmosphere of corruption and decay.'

Caretaker came to an end. Theodora allowed him a few moments and then she said, gently, 'There is, is there not, one further element? Between you and the Bishop?'

Ian paused before answering and then said, 'I knew the Bishop's son, Thomas junior. Dhani and I both did. He was a year above me at school and at Cambridge. He was heavily into drugs by the time he left school and carried on at Cambridge.' Ian's voice was laden with pain. 'I think I know the reason for his death and I think I could have stopped it. I also think Bishop Thomas knows this and does not, cannot, forgive me, as I do not forgive myself.'

He stopped talking. The tiny river sounds came in through the open hatches. The light had quite gone now and they were bound together in the glow which came from the lantern above their heads.

After a while Theodora said, 'My own contribution here will be more circumstantial. If we want to find out who killed Paul Gray, and why, we need to focus both on his character and on the parish in which he served. My impression is that just before his death Paul Gray was under some sort of pressure. As you know I visited his widow last week and she seemed to hint at pressure coming from two areas: the youth leader Jefferson and Canon Wheeler. She was not precise as to the nature of Gray's relationship with either. After I had seen her, I visited the church and found on the altar a candle bearing the arms of the Cathedral on its base. As Ian knows these candles are provided for the Cathedral's use alone. They are expensive. Their numbers are known and supposedly accounted for by the vergers. Later, when I visited the vice-chairman of the PCC, who is also the vicar's warden, he could give me no explanation of why the candle was there. But he did allow me to examine it and bring it away with me. I showed it to you this morning Ian. I think we are agreed, are we not, that it may be connected with the one which you and Julia found in the asylum out-buildings?'

Theodora pressed on, 'What the vicar's warden also told me was that Paul had become more and more involved with the Youth Club and, in particular, with Jefferson, who had worked with him at Narborough. Jefferson is one of those people upon whom Church youth groups seem often to depend. He has contacts, access to halls, knew where there were vans for hire, cheap sports equipment, that sort of thing. I get the impression that the warden was impressed without actually liking the man. He said he was good particularly with the tough boys. "Charismatic" was the word he first used and later withdrew — apparently on the grounds that Jefferson's personality, while it is undoubtedly attractive to teenagers, isn't particularly pleasant. His last remark to me was that if there was any jiggery-pokery about candles he wouldn't be at all surprised if Jefferson didn't have a hand in it. I really don't know, and the man certainly wasn't telling, whether he had any hard evidence at all to connect Jefferson with the theft, if it was a theft, of candles from the Cathedral. And, if it was stolen, why should Paul Gray connive, if he did connive, by using it in his church?'

'Is the candle at Paul's church connected with the one Julia and I found at the asylum out-house? I mean they both had the Cathedral arms on them. What do you think, Dhani?' asked Ian turning to his friend.

'I wonder if perhaps there is some possibility of black magic which needed Cathedral candles.'

'And would there be a connection, then, between the magic ritual and the murder of Paul, and placing his head in a font?' asked Julia.

'I suppose Jefferson could be connected with a magic ritual which made use of Cathedral candles,' Ian said speculatively.

'Jefferson was on Canon Wheeler's hit list,' Julia said suddenly. Theodora raised a questioning eyebrow and Julia told Dhani and Theodora about the list of five names on the sheets which had fallen from Canon Wheeler's copy of *Crockford*.

'So we have five names on that list,' said Dhani. 'Paul Gray, Ian, Jefferson, Williams the verger, and Markham, the son of Cumbermound — your acquaintance Ian. What is their connection with each other and with Wheeler and with the murder and the two candles?'

'Could Wheeler be involved with selling candles for use in black magic?' asked Julia.

'Oh come,' Theodora murmured.

'Wheeler certainly knew or suspected something about candles since he's been questioning Williams about them,' said Ian, recalling his unsatisfactory conversation with the Verger. 'Though of course he might just have been making routine checks. Williams would certainly have access to candles,' he continued. 'I wonder if the line of candle leaks might not be from Williams to Jefferson to Paul. The question would then be: who knew how much *en route*? It seems a bit unlikely that Paul would use candles which he would know he had no right to use or that he would actually be involved in magic practices.'

'Though Canon Wheeler apparently thought he had something on Paul. Enough to make his life a misery,' Dhani said.

'It sounds as though Wheeler was pursuing his old course of the row over the youth club at Narborough and trying to make out Paul's part was more dishonourable than the Archdeacon and the Bishop said it was. "A Bishop's favourite" were the words Wheeler wrote on the *Crockford* list,' Theodora pointed out.

'What can we do?' asked Julia, suddenly tired. 'I can't believe that Paul was a black magician. I don't really care if he was a homosexual — though I'd rather his taste were for adults. And I don't want to think he was mean enough to pick up stolen candles from a crooked verger.'

'And then there is always the problem of Markham,' said Dhani, looking at Ian.

'My own feeling would be,' Theodora said crisply, 'that it might help us to find out in more detail what Paul's movements were immediately before his death. The best lead we have here is the one given by his wife. She thought that the day he was murdered he received a letter which, she guessed from his reaction to it, was from Canon Wheeler. A fact, by the way, she had not communicated to the police. We need to know whether Paul got to the Cathedral under his own steam and at what time. And where he went.'

'How do you propose to find that out?' asked Ian. 'Interrogate Wheeler?' The edge of hatred showed in his tone.

'No,' said Theodora. 'I'm inclined to think that we need to break into the Cathedral's conspiracy of silence, since the police clearly won't be able to. I shall approach the Archdeacon's wife, Moira Baggley. There's such a good view from her window.'

CHAPTER SEVEN: PASTORAL PLEASURES

'What you're telling me, Tallboy,' said the Superintendent with practised distaste, 'is that the sum total of knowledge gleaned by almost the entire Medewich police force, continuously engaged over the last ten days comes to this: Paul Gray was murdered on Thursday or Friday July first or second, somewhere between Markham cum Cumbermound and Medewich, by persons unknown, at a time not yet established, at a place not yet identified, for an as yet undiscovered reason. Not, if I may say so, a very riveting tale to tell the coroner.'

Inspector Tallboy didn't know the precise meaning of the word 'gleaned', but he caught the general tone. He'd always admired his superior and never more so than when a victim of his contempt. He looked forward to practising it himself on others in due course. He could, however, think of better ways of spending a fine Sunday morning. 'We've got the murder weapon, sir,' he said humbly.

'Yes, and thanks to the Dean's Beagle bitch, we know where the body was hidden.'

'Labrador, sir,' said Tallboy accurately, 'black Labrador.'

'What?'

'Black Labrador bitch, sir.'

'Well, perhaps you'd better enrol her. She certainly seems to have done a lot more than your lot.'

'It'd be handy if we could question her, sir.'

'Don't be flippant, Tallboy.'

The Superintendent leaned back in the chair in the diocesan office conference room, Tallboy sitting opposite. Superintendent Frost was a small, dapper, acute little man, with the trace of a Scottish accent and a grey moustache which his subordinates said he was able, when angry, to make bristle like a dog's hackles.

'Let's go over it again, Inspector,' said the Superintendent with summoned kindliness. 'On Thursday the first of July, after Evensong in his church at Markham cum Cumbermound for a congregation of two, at about five fifteen, Paul Gray stepped back to the Vicarage for a sandwich and a glass of milk before going into Medewich to fetch Mr Jefferson of Markham Terrace who, as was his practice, was going to help Gray with his youth club in Markham cum Cumbermound. According to Mr Jefferson, he did not turn up in Medewich.'

'Our inquiries,' interposed Tallboy unwisely, 'at Markham Terrace have suggested that no one saw him arrive. I think it is safe to assume . . .' His voice trailed off as he caught the Superintendent's eye.

'Do go on,' said the Superintendent dangerously.

'Well, we haven't found his car either,' concluded Tallboy.

'Just so. Perhaps the Beagle, sorry, Labrador, could help you.'

Tallboy felt he'd had enough of that one.

'What about the weapon?' invited the Superintendent.

'Well, sir, the forensic people say there are traces of blood of the same group as Gray's, rhesus negative' — he consulted his notes — 'A, on the inside of the scabbard and on the hilt. Not much, but enough to be sure. The sword itself is the ceremonial sword of Major the Honourable Clement Braithwaite, who was killed at Peshawar. In India, sir,' he added earnestly.

The Superintendent shuddered, 'In 1840, while serving with the Medewich and Markham Light Infantry. The sword was presented by the family to the Cathedral chapel when it was dedicated in 1927. And are you able to tell me, Inspector, how a hundred-and-fifty-year-old dress sword came to be sharp enough to sever a man's head?'

'Well, the difficulty is we don't know when the sword was taken. Though, if Caretaker is right, we do know when it was returned. Our only witness is the Cathedral cleaner, Mrs Thrigg, who thinks, but isn't sure, that it was in its place on the Tuesday before the murder when she cleaned round the pews in the infantry chapel.'

'Vergers?'

'Couldn't say for sure.'

'Clergy?'

'The chapel isn't used for any regular services and they aren't a terribly observant body of men, if you see what I mean.'

'So, sometime before or during the course of Thursday evening, a ceremonial sword is taken from its place in the Infantry chapel, sharpened and applied to the head of a priest. On Friday, at approximately quarter past three in the afternoon, the head is found in the font of the Cathedral by Mrs Miranda Thrigg and Miss Julia Smith. The sword is returned to the Cathedral the following Thursday at about two o'clock in the morning. Why?'

'Why what, sir?'

'Why was the sword returned? I mean, it was a lot of trouble to return it. Why do it?'

'Quite frankly, sir, I haven't got the foggiest idea.'

The Superintendent didn't look as though this came as a surprise to him. 'It smacks of ritual, wouldn't you say, Inspector? It is a flourish, the action of someone with a sense of style, of form. It suggests the gesture was a symbolic one. But what would it be symbolising, I wonder, and to whom?'

'You mean like a soldier's salute, sir?'

The Superintendent eyed the Inspector speculatively. 'You surprise me, Inspector, with your acumen.'

The Inspector was fairly sure acumen was a good thing to have.

'Let's think about the body, Inspector. The body, too, may have its symbolic significance. It was placed in the compost heap of the Dean's house, when?'

'Well, that's difficult, sir. Apparently forensic want to argue that the head was severed from the body after death. The neck was probably broken first. They say the body was probably in the compost for about a week. That makes sense, but they can't be accurate because compost heaps generate heat which might accelerate decomposition. So we don't know whether the body was put into the compost at the same time as the head was put into the font or before it or after.'

'Dating problems are always complex, Inspector. So, we lack both a time and a place for the murder. Was anything found on the body, papers of any kind?'

'No papers. A wallet with about seven pounds in it.'

'Car keys?'

'No.'

'So someone took his keys but not his wallet. Did his wife or anyone actually see Gray start out in his car?'

'His little lad, his son, Paul, did. He's a bit young of course, but a bright boy. Quite coherent and certain he saw his dad make a phone call from the instrument in the hall and then drive off in the car. He's not sure of the time but he says it was after he'd eaten his sandwich, say six in the evening. The only other sighting we've had was a farm worker who thought he saw the car up towards Cumbermound about nine. But he wasn't sure and we've searched every inch of the ground with no result.'

'Do we know who Gray made the phone call to?'

'No. The boy doesn't know. Gray ought to have been cancelling his youth club, which he usually held on a Thursday evening. But he didn't do that. Some of the lads turned up.'

'So he went off in such a hurry or so worried that he forgot to cancel. Did he receive any phone calls that day?'

'Mrs Gray thinks he had a number in the morning but doesn't know who they were from. Trade in that direction for a parish priest is fairly brisk, arrangements for christenings, funerals, marriages, that sort of thing,' Tallboy said offhandedly, as though he himself regularly joined couples in wedlock.

'So he went out in a hurry. Where did he go?'

'The Cathedral.'

'You deduce this on the grounds that his head and body ended up there?'

'I suppose he could have been done in somewhere else and then carted up there.'

'Forensics?'

'They don't show us that he'd been anywhere he might not be expected to have been, if you see what I mean. For example, there was an oil smear on his jacket of the same type as what he used in his car. Gravel on the shoes that could have come from the Cathedral. There's only one odd thing.'

The Superintendent raised an eyebrow.

'There are splinters of polished mahogany under the fingernails of the right hand.'

'From his own house?'

'Impossible to say for certain, sir. Though I did notice that there was pine and oak in his house and not mahogany.'

'You're very observant, Inspector.'

'My dad was a boat builder, sir,' said Tallboy modestly.

'But we don't know where he went to get his splinters?'

Tallboy shook his head.

'And that, of course, leaves us with the problem of motive. Have we turned up any, Inspector?'

'It's tricky. We've taken statements from both ends, Cathedral and village. Frankly, the Cathedral's a nightmare. The clergy either notice nothing or they aren't telling. They seem to think they're special in some way, almost as though they had the right to choose whether they'll cooperate or not.' Tallboy's baffled resentment at their attitude showed in his tone.

Frost smiled grimly. 'Think before they answer your questions, do they?' He could imagine the unfamiliarity of such an approach to a policeman used to witnesses who worked on the fairly simple patterns of response found on the Cumbermound council estate.

'You could say that, sir. It's almost like a club and we're not members. I don't get the feeling that they particularly care whether this murder is solved or not; anyway they want it solved on their terms and if it's going to muddy a lot of their holy bloody waters they'd like us to go away. The general attitude seems to be that it must have been a madman and the Church doesn't have to deal with madmen. Only nice ordinary sane ones.'

'What about the village?'

'The difficulty there is that absolutely everyone wants to talk — a great deal. I'd no idea that the parson was so visible, if you see what I mean.'

Frost did.

'Everyone, whether they go to church or not, seems to have some knowledge of Reverend Gray's character and circumstances. Him and his wife both. The villagers seem to be half for, half against him. The main criticism seems to be that he wanted to change things, forms of service and such like. The other half were in favour of him *because* he wanted to change things.' Tallboy thought about what he had said but then battled on. 'Of course he was a bit young, only twenty-nine. And it was his first parish. Apparently they're supposed to do two curacies before they get one of their own, but this chap was a bit of a favourite of the Bishop and the Bishop is patron of the living.'

'Quite a dab hand at the clerical jargon, aren't you, Tallboy?'

'I try to be accurate, sir,' said the Inspector modestly. 'Actually the Archdeacon was kind enough to fill me in on that aspect of things. He, Gray, that is, not the Archdeacon, came originally from Wolverhampton. Ordinary family. Father an accountant. Father and mother both dead. Started to train as an accountant after leaving the local comprehensive. Gave it up for ordination training at Salisbury. Married at twenty-two a woman eleven years older than himself, with one son by a previous marriage. Widow not divorced. One son of seven by her. Did his first and only curacy at Narborough in the port area.'

'Yes, yes, yes,' the Superintendent muttered.

'Well, sir, it's not so irrelevant because while he was in that curacy there was some sort of row about a boy in the youth club. Quite what, I'm not certain. I started by assuming it was the usual sort of thing but I've made inquiries with our people in Narborough and I'm not sure it was anything sexual. Or not straightforwardly so anyway.'

The Inspector was a local boy, not a sophisticated metropolitan cop, and he liked his vice straightforward. He wasn't sure what he'd found out or how to phrase it. He was red and sweating slightly as he went on.

'We haven't been able to get hold of the boy concerned since he and his family moved away soon after the incident, whatever it was. There were no police statements taken and the thing never even looked like coming to court. The Church, the vicar and the Archdeacon and the Bishop all weighed in on Gray's side so it was quietly dropped and he got his parish here a year later. However, the tale seems to have followed him, because I gather some of his parishioners certainly thought he had deviant tendencies in spite of his having a wife and son. On the other hand, no parent that we questioned voiced any suspicions with regard to their own children and they all seemed quite happy for them to attend his youth club. Very popular it was and the parents were glad to have their kids taken off their hands. Especially in a village like Markham cum Cumbermound with nothing to do for kids in the evening.'

'And what do you suppose,' said the Superintendent heavily, 'is the connection between the man's sexual deviance, if he had one, and his severed head?'

'I honestly don't know, sir, unless one of the parents . . . ?'

'I thought you said none of them did.'

'They could be concealing it. But I don't know that actually killing a man because he's been touching up the boys would altogether hang together as a motive.'

'How about the head?'

'How about it, sir?'

'Given that an angry parent might just conceivably break Gray's neck for, as you put it, touching up his youngster, why should he go to the trouble of severing the head, and then putting it in the Cathedral font? Why should he be farsighted enough to steal and sharpen a ceremonial sword to do it with? And why should he take the trouble to return the said sword to the Cathedral afterwards?'

'A nutter, sir,' said Tallboy readily.

The Superintendent sighed. 'That, of course, obviates the need for us even to attempt to detect or frame coherent theories of motivation. Dammit, Tallboy, even given the poverty of your mind and the inadequacy of police training nowadays, surely they must have taught you that madmen, nutters, as you call them, follow a pattern? Their actions are meaningful to themselves and therefore to us. All we need to do is to widen — or invert — our normal frames of reference.'

Tallboy continued to sweat. There was quite a lot he didn't follow in his Superintendent's speech starting with 'obviate'. Still, he caught the general tone.

'Well, I don't know why anyone should go to that trouble. Too fancy as you say, sir,' he said placatorily.

'Orpheus, of course, lost his head,' said the Superintendent ruminatively, the Scottish accent now quite discernible.

Tallboy scanned the list of people from whom statements had been taken. It ran from 'Caretaker I' to 'Williams J'. 'Who, sir?' he asked desperately.

'Orpheus rejected women so they tore him to pieces and threw his head into the River Hebrus. It wasn't that he didn't like women, you understand, he simply stayed faithful to one who was dead. He became a cult figure in which notions of salvation by innocent suffering have a place. An interesting pagan anticipation of later Christian teaching. Would that make sense in a Cathedral setting, eh Tallboy?'

Tallboy played safe. 'It might, sir, it might indeed,' he added. God knew what the Superintendent was on about.

'And then perhaps,' conceded the Superintendent, 'there was our own St Manicus, killed, as legend has it, by a madman who thought himself an executioner.'

'That's quite right, sir,' said Tallboy with relief. He'd heard about St Manicus: they'd done a project on him at school.

'On the other hand,' said Frost, 'rather more straight-forwardly, down to the end of the seventeenth century, severing the head was the penalty for treachery. Would any of that make sense to a twentieth-century madman, a nutter, eh, Tallboy?'

'It might, sir, it might indeed.' Personally, he just hoped it was some headcase from the funny farm up the hill who'd been let out on parole too early with a meat axe. No dammit, they knew the weapon. With the sword, then. The dress sword of Major the Honourable etc. Him of India.

'We're checking the asylum people, of course,' he said, 'to see if they've got anyone in who might have these sorts of—', he hesitated '—propensities.' It seemed to go down all right so he cleared his throat. 'These sorts of propensities,' he reiterated more confidently. 'Or alternatively anyone who they released recently with similar ones. They'll let us know when they've checked their records.' Or, he added privately, when the little Indian gentleman who was the only one who could access the records on the computer returned from sick leave.

'A sound move, Inspector.'

Tallboy wasn't sure how to judge his superior's tone but he needed a fillip to his esteem right now so he looked on the bright side. 'Thank you, sir.'

'And now,' said the Superintendent carefully, 'I'd like you to get out your notebook, and make a list of the things I want you to do. First, Mrs Thrigg and then Mr Jefferson . . .'

* * *

'Four faults,' crackled the public address system as the little bright-bay mare failed to tuck her hind feet up quite high enough at the last bar of the treble.

'Jolly well ridden, Dolly,' said Georgina Landsdown to Laura Medaware, her cousin by marriage.

'She's really come on quite a lot this season with the help of Alison Midsummer,' said Dolly's mother with modest pride. A desultory round of applause marked the end of the jump-off.

Lord Cumbermound revolved on his shooting stick in the direction of the two women. 'That bay's too small for her now, Georgina,' he said genially. 'If that gelding of yours is any good, I'll put my hand in my pocket for him for Dolly. She's worth backing on her present form.'

Georgina smiled back companionably, 'Oh, he's a smart pony, all right. I think he and Dolly'd get on a treat.'

Laura Medaware put the remains of her gin and tonic in its plastic cup down by her canvas chair, ground her menthol cigarette into the turf and said, 'Come on, Georgina. Come and hold a bridle and have a word with Dolly. She always values your praise.'

The two women, one tall, middle-aged and handsome, the other smaller, younger and compact, wove their way amongst the debris of cups and chairs which littered the grass. They picked their way carefully over the leads of numerous Labradors, terriers and springers anchored with more or less acquiescence, to bits of their owners' persons. Avoiding the attentions of small, clamorous children with food and drink in their hands they made their way out of the members enclosure of the Medewich and Markham Agricultural Show.

Now, late on Sunday afternoon, people were saying that the weather had been perfect for both days of the two-day Show. Lord Cumbermound, a lucky gambler, had pointed out that he usually got good weather for his show.

'You carry on as though you controlled the weather George,' his cousin, the Dean had said with acerbity.

'Like God,' had added his profane wife.

'Perfect weather, perfect setting,' his lordship had asserted with no trace of boastfulness. He loved his house, his estate, his horses, his county and his country. He saw no reason not to enjoy them all and he was quite generous enough to share his enjoyment with others by providing, once a year, a venue for the Show.

The park sloped down gently from his undistinguished seventeenth-century brick house, the grandest part of which was the stable block, to the lake below. The Show was held in the meadows on the higher ground on the opposite side of the lake. The house looked as it had done for three centuries; Lord Cumbermound was in no doubt that it would manage another three.

In the goat tent Julia stood beside Ian. She was enjoying herself hugely. 'The trouble with Saanans is, they all look alike,' she announced.

Ian was in no position to disagree with her. He'd admitted early on that he'd never looked closely at goats before. He'd liked, therefore, the flashy Nubians with their grotesque, bloodhound ears and patronising expressions.

'Too refined,' Julia explained didactically and pressed on to introduce him to the black and white humbug types labelled British Alpines, standing next to the skewbald variety called British Toggenbergs. Ian liked the names and was content to scratch the animals' heads as, emitting a warm goaty smell, they gazed up at him with calculating yellow eyes.

'The cloven hoof is very marked,' he said happily in parody of the judge's comments.

'I think this is the nicest thing that's happened to me in England,' said Julia with real contentment. 'I'd no idea you carried on like this. It's all so natural.'

In contrast to what? Ian wondered. To the Chapter and Cathedral, to the diocesan office? To his eyes, the Show had its conventions and artificialities too. But then he supposed, it was a question of what one was used to: artificialities struck a stranger so much more strongly.

Having exhausted the goats they moved via pigs, pigeons, game birds and Burmese cats to the main ring.

'I'd quite like to see the final judging of the handy hunter,' said Julia knowledgeably. Here their interests lay closer together. Ian had ridden as a boy and he suspected from the way Julia commented that, although she was socially timid, she might be an efficient horsewoman. They came up in time to see the penultimate line-up. It consisted of a grey, with black tack ('Very vulgar,' said Ian to see how Julia would react; she made no answer) and a large handsome chestnut mare with good shoulders but long in the back and with that slightly dotty look in her eye usual in chestnut mares. Then came two bays, a light and a dark. The dark bay was a seventeen-hand mare, perhaps young, beautifully conformed, with a kind eye and immaculately turned out.

'Have they ridden them?' asked Julia.

'I think all of them except the dark bay.'

Julia's eye glittered. She watched as the bowler-hatted judge patted the mare's neck and prepared to mount. Clearly it was a moment with its own significance for her. The judge swung himself calmly into the saddle and the mare stood without moving while he adjusted his stirrups. There was a moment's quietness, as of a grace before a meal, and then the mare stepped sweetly forward from leg to hand. The aid had been invisible. The judge was a good rider in the old-fashioned seat, legs slightly too far forward for the modern taste but with the body nice and upright, hands quiet and soft. Although not a young man, there was, nevertheless, nothing stiff or cramped about him. The mare started to track up and softened to the bit. She settled to her walk and began to swing her quarters. Halfway round the ring when he asked for little more collection she offered no resistance and they moved as one into an easy working trot rising.

Julia could not take her eyes off the beautiful mare. At the quarter marker he asked for canter and got extended trot. Well, she's young yet, she thought, and that leg of his was so far forward the mare could easily make a mistake. The rider seemed to sense the fault was partly his. He tried again at the corner and got a smooth rounded canter. Julia wondered if he would gallop her: surely he must for a hunter class. She watched as the mare completed a second circuit in canter, waiting for her rider to ask for the gallop. She was a large animal and any minute now, Julia thought, he would be holding her up. However, the rider's feel for the mare was sure. He closed his legs and she came smoothly into a nice even gallop. He wisely asked for the downward transition after a circuit and the mare came down to trot, threw her head up briefly and then rounded again. Julia let out her breath. He circled her in a 20-metre circle, changed the rein through two half-circles and repeated the performance on the left rein. The halt, when he asked for it, was square.

'Very, very pleasant,' said Ian, at one with Julia in admiration of the performance.

'Whose is she?' asked Julia.

Ian consulted the programme. 'Number 15, Rosa, Geoffrey Markham. That's Cumbermound's youngest son.'

'And who is riding her?'

Ian looked again. 'Judges: Mrs Henrietta Gibson and Major L. Braithwaite. That's Theodora's uncle, I think.'

When Julia looked again at the judge, she could see the family likeness. The long square head came out well in the male version. 'Yes, he rides a bit like Theodora: kind and competent. He's sensitive to the horse, without all that macho pushing and pulling you sometimes get in male riders.'

They watched as the judges conferred and then placed them in order in the line-up. Rosa was called in second, the grey first, the chestnut and light bay third and fourth.

'Very satisfactory,' said Julia incisively. 'Ian,' she added suddenly, 'I'm not going to go on being a poor typist to people I dislike and am frightened of. I'm going to get a job as a farm worker.'

Ian was amused. 'They last had land girls during the war. Green jerseys and breeches. I had an aunt in the trade. I've got photographs of her leaning on hay rakes with yokels in smocks, more or less.'

The war was not a concept which claimed Julia's attention anymore than land girls. 'How would I go about it? I mean getting a job on the land?'

'Oh, come on, Julia. Women don't work on the land in this country. You must know that. Come to think of it, not many men work on it either. It's all done with tractors and computers.'

Julia assumed that mutinous expression which Ian had seen on her face when having her work returned to her by Miss Coldharbour. As in that situation, she said nothing. He hadn't meant to bully her. He hadn't realised she was so serious. He was contrite. 'I'm sorry,' he said. 'Let's go and get some tea and perhaps we might make inquiries about types of jobs amongst the local farmers. We'd better hurry, though, they'll be striking camp ere long.'

They threaded their way round the ring towards the tea tent. Halfway round they met Theodora walking with her uncle in the direction of the members enclosure. Theodora lifted an eyebrow and with a caught glance drew them in to introductions.

Major Braithwaite and Julia started talking about horses. There was a sort of thirstiness about Julia's immersion in the conversation, as though she'd been parched for a long time. Theodora watched her, with pleasure. She and Ian drew a little apart from the two of them.

'Julia wants to chuck typing and be a land girl,' Ian said to Theodora.

'That would probably be best,' replied Theodora in her pastoral voice. 'She's not happy in the office. She's both too intelligent and too incompetent to flourish in that setting.'

'Would you suppose she'd be more competent on the land? How would her intelligence survive hoeing cabbages?'

'They don't hoe now, they spray, unfortunately. Anyway, she might do something with horses, by the sound of it,' said Theodora.

'Would that exercise her intelligence?'

'Oh, yes,' said Theodora. 'I'm sure you know it's one of the Zen arts. Body and spirit are both totally engaged and concentrated. My uncle's instincts are just as religious as my father's and mine in his way.'

They turned back to Major Braithwaite who was talking to Julia with what, in so staid a man, was approaching animation. 'I wonder if you'd care to come up to the stable at the house and help me box a pair of geldings of mine?' he was inquiring. 'I brought them over yesterday and George let me have a couple of boxes for the night but I don't want to leave them over another night if I can help it. If you like big bays, you'd like my boy Oscar. He's a fine fellow. Knight's not a bad chap either.'

Julia was clearly on the point of accepting but remembering her manners pointed out that since Ian had brought her she could hardly desert him.

'I'd love to help box your horses, Major,' said Ian swiftly. 'I'm not too knowledgeable, but I can do as I'm told.'

Julia looked delighted.

They began to walk down the hill towards the lake. Skirting the marshy end, they slowly climbed the gentle slope on the other side to join the carriage drive which led them to the stable. As they stepped from grass to gravel, a long dark green Mercedes two-seater swept towards them, accelerating fast. Julia caught a glimpse of a small, neat head, a younger version of the Earl behind the steering wheel. Ian watched the progress of the car down the drive and Major Braithwaite raised his hand in a brief, unacknowledged greeting before the Mercedes raced out of sight.

The stable block had been built later than the house, in the mid-eighteenth century. It was set around a complete quadrangle and built of rusticated stone. The tall carriage entrance had a clock with a black face and gilt Roman numerals in its small pediment, the yard paved with small, sunk cobbles with moss between. There was a wellhead in the middle, mounting blocks round three sides and fourteen boxes, six of which were in use. A tack room and hay loft took up the north side; on the south side were grooms' and coachman's quarters. A better working environment than the diocesan office, Julia thought, as she surveyed it. Better designed too.

The yard was empty except for a neat looking two-horse box and at the far end a large powerful motorbike. Major Braithwaite approached the box and undid the pins to release the tail gate.

'My girl, Helen, landed on the deck a bit heavily in the jump-off of the Foxhunter and had to go home early, so I'm without labour at the moment. Hence, glad of your help. Glad of it anyhow,' he added as if caught out in some discourtesy.

Ian grinned. He'd forgotten how much he knew the ways of horsemen of old.

'I think I'm about ready to load. Theo, can you take Oscar and I'll follow up with Knight? Ian, if you and Julia stand by to raise the bridge, I think we'll do very nicely. Knight's sometimes a bit nervous about all this. He's still new to the travelling.'

Theodora and the Major moved off to collect the horses from the loose boxes at the north end of the yard. Theodora emerged leading a bay gelding of about sixteen hands. Irish draft with a trace of Cleveland, thought Julia watching the selfish, handsome head as he surveyed the box without fear and walked calmly up the ramp beside Theodora into the left-hand stall. The Major followed close behind with what was clearly a horse of a different stamp. He was a thorough-bred, lighter, therefore, of bone, his thin chiselled head evincing distrust of the strange machine in front of him. At the foot of the ramp he stopped dead. The Major encouraged him, then walked him round in a circle, conversing with him in low reassuring tones. Again the horse refused, his nostrils flaring with fear and his eyes appearing to swivel back under his ears.

'Ian,' said the Major calmly, 'I think I can make out his saddle on the block over there. Could you bring it over and we'll saddle him up? Julia, his bridle, I think, must still be in the tack room. His is a 5-inch French link with rubber reins on the peg to the left of the door.'

Julia shot off in the direction of the tack room. When she reached it, it was empty. She stood in the doorway, taking in the lofty whitewashed space with match-boarding to shoulder height and saddle racks full of Stubens and Passats, all clean. Julia breathed the incense of saddle soap and neatsfoot oil appreciatively. A 5-inch French link with rubber reins to the left of the door, the Major had said. There were two double bridles and a fixed ring snaffle. Hell she thought, where, oh, where was it? Julia scanned the rest of the pegs. Nothing like. At the far end of the room, next to the sink was a deal table. On the table were two grooming kit boxes, a couple of 'L' plates, a discarded car number plate and, thank Heaven, the unassembled pieces of a bridle with a 5-inch French link bit on it. Julia was halfway through assembling the bridle when she stopped short. She caught her breath. She looked again. There was no mistaking it. SVF 907. Being one of those who makes words out of initials, Julia, when first shown that number by the police, had changed mentally the V to U, as in the Latin alphabet, and came up with SUF, the first syllable of 'suffer', which, she'd thought at the time, were appropriate registration letters for her cousin Paul Gray's car, missing now for nearly two weeks.

Julia picked up the plate and turned it over. What on earth was it doing here and what on earth should she do about it? Her first thought, she realised, was that she hated the idea of the police trampling all over this heaven on earth. Her second feeling was pity for her murdered and mutilated cousin and her third feeling was one of fear. She turned round quickly as she heard the sound of a step at the door. It was Ian.

'I thought you might be having difficulty spotting . . .' he began. Then he caught sight of her face. 'What's up?'

She indicated the number plate on the table. Caretaker glanced at it. Then he too perceived what she meant. Everyone questioned by the police (and Julia and Ian had been questioned twice) knew the registration of Gray's car. Had they seen it? When had it last been parked in the Cathedral car park? Did Gray have a parking permit? How long had he had this particular car? And so on. Ian, who was responsible for dealing with diocesan loans to incumbents for cars, had had to go into some detail on these points.

Julia realised that she was shaking and that Ian had taken her hand in his. 'Do nothing now,' he said firmly. 'We'll box the horses and I'll drive you back to *Amy Roy*. We'll talk about it there.'

'You have a horseman's priorities,' said Julia, laughing nervously. 'First box the horses.'

'I was a prominent member of the pony club,' said Ian with equal lameness. 'Anyway, we might be mistaken about the registration number. I ought to check up before we set hounds on.'

They both knew, however, that there was no mistake.

Julia took up the assembled bridle and they walked outside into the early evening sun. The sheer beauty of the handsome yard revived her. Standing beside Major Braithwaite's box were the Dean, the Dean's wife, Lord Cumbermound, his daughter and granddaughter, the latter in jodhpurs, blue shirt and the horrible purple and green of the pony club tie. There was that confident murmur of well-bred voices which Julia was beginning to associate with a certain sort of English gathering.

A flash of recognition crossed the Earl's face as he lit on Julia. 'Hello, me dear,' he said affably. 'Been over fences?'

Julia managed a smile, 'Not yet,' she said and added, 'Your mare Rosa's very beautiful.'

Cumbermound looked pleased. 'Is she not?' he said. 'Found her on half an acre in Buckinghamshire with her mother and got her for my youngest lad. Have you met him? Geoffrey, I mean.'

'No, I don't know him.'

'He was here a bit earlier. You just missed him. You know Geoffrey, Caretaker, don't you?' said Cumbermound unexpectedly swinging round to Ian.

Ian for once looked thoroughly discomposed. He had not realised that Lord Cumbermound had recognised him.

'Yes, I know your son slightly,' he said stiffly. 'We met at Cambridge once or twice.'

'And after that, I gather,' said his father, 'in London.'

Julia looked at Ian in surprise. He was as embarrassed as she had ever seen him.

'Yes,' said Ian almost sulkily. There was an awkward pause. For a moment Julia thought that Ian was going to walk away. Then the girl, Dolly, suddenly started to caper. 'Can I lead Knight up the ramp, Theo? He'll come for me.'

Theodora handed over the reins of the now saddled and bridled Knight who had begun to fear that he was no longer the centre of attention. The girl held them in approved BHS fashion.

'Now, Knight,' Dolly said firmly. 'Don't be a pain. You've known me for yonks.' She marched him in an exact 15-metre circle. With no hesitation he stepped on to the ramp and into the right-hand stall of the horse box.

'And a little child shall lead them,' murmured the Dean's wife.

* * *

'I've got one thing to tell you and one favour to ask of you,' Ian said to Julia the minute they got back to the *Amy Roy*. 'The favour is that we don't tell the police immediately about the car number plate. It's Sunday today. If I haven't made any headway by Tuesday morning, I'll go to the police and tell them about the plate. How about it?'

'Well,' said Julia, 'it depends on what else you have to tell me. And, of course, what I want to know most of all is why Paul's number plate happened to be in Lord Cumbermound's stable.'

Ian hesitated and then said slowly, 'The number plate links Paul to Geoffrey Markham, Cumbermound's youngest son.'

'The boy we saw driving out in the Mercedes tourer. Rosa's owner? How do you know? It could be anyone at Cumbermound's house.'

'All right then. It's only intuition. But say there is a link between Paul and Markham, what would the link most likely be?'

'How on earth should I know?' Julia cried in irritation. 'I gathered it was you who had a previous acquaintance with him.'

'It wouldn't be sex, Markham never had any "problems" in that direction, so to speak. With him it's likely to be money in the end.'

'How "in the end"?'

'Well, something might lie between.'

'Like?'

'Candles,' said Ian thoughtfully.

'I don't see it.'

'Neither do I at the moment,' Ian admitted. 'But before I go I'll have a look at the one I found in the asylum and the one Theodora got from Paul's church.'

'Go?' said Julia. 'Go where? Where are you going?'

'Rosamund Coldharbour's.'

'Miss Coldharbour's? What on earth are you going there for?'

'Both Markham and Paul figure on Wheeler's hit list don't they?'

'So? Williams and Jefferson are on it too.'

'But Jefferson and Williams have had no opportunity to have their hands in the Cathedral till. If my financial researches are right I have to say the most likely suspect for that particular activity is Wheeler.'

Julia nodded.

'If I'm right and the link is money, who knows most about Wheeler's financial affairs?'

'I suppose she would.'

'Say Markham is paying Wheeler or Wheeler is paying Markham for services rendered and say Paul was implicated either way, might not Rosamund know about it, if it involved money going into or out of any of Wheeler's accounts?'

'I suppose so,' said Julia. 'But would she tell you if she did know? She's terrifically loyal to Canon Wheeler.'

‘That will depend on how clever my questioning is and on how frightened she can be made to feel either for herself or on Wheeler’s behalf.’

‘And it depends on what her relations with Wheeler are,’ said Julia with gathering interest.

‘And no one quite knows the answer to that one, do they? Reason enough for me to try my luck with her.’

Half an hour later Julia agreed the police should not be told about the number plate until Tuesday.

‘I don’t think there’s the least danger to you,’ said Ian reassuringly as they parted.

CHAPTER EIGHT: THINE ADVERSARY THE DEVIL

Tallboy rang the bell of 27, Markham Terrace. One of these tubular affairs, he noticed, ever so discreet. He curbed a wish to kick his boot against the bottle-glass panels of the front door. The house was one of a row of nineteenth-century brick artisan dwellings whose neat and harmonious proportions were now being ruined as recent prosperity allowed the enlargement of windows and the addition of porches, complete with brass carriage lamps and, Tallboy thought vindictively, bloody tubular bells. He raised his fist and was about to hammer on the door when he heard sounds. A moment later there was a rattling of chains and locks and the door swung open.

Tallboy was confronted by a very tall man of considerable girth who looked like a retired all-in wrestler. His thick, almost grey hair appeared to be worn without a parting and stopped at the lobes of his ears. He wore a light-blue, Fair Isle pullover, fawn slacks and grey trainers.

'Mr Jefferson?'

The man smiled slowly and in no hurry at all replied softly, 'The very same.'

'I'm Inspector Tallboy of Medewich CID. I'm engaged in investigating the murder of the Reverend Paul Gray. We have your statement taken earlier this week by Sergeant Bison. But I wondered whether I could ask you one or two further questions?'

The man continued to smile and then, with a quick, balanced movement, which in so bulky a man was nimble, he moved backwards and sideways to allow Tallboy through the narrow porch into the house. The Inspector edged down the confined passage into the living room which looked out on to a neat back garden. French windows stood open leading on to a strip of highly polished, red tiled terrace.

The room was carpeted in a very thick fawn carpet with a wave-like configuration in its pile. The furniture of the 1930s was beautifully preserved. Over the mottled beige tiled mantel piece, with its brass jar filled with coloured spills, was a glass case of military cap badges mounted in wooden frames. Tallboy eased himself into the atmosphere. When he saw the cap badges he felt himself to be on home ground. He might not know much about the Church, but with this terrain he was thoroughly familiar. He knew what he'd find in the wardrobe upstairs if he ever had to search the place. He did not need to look at the single shelf of books to know they would have titles like *A Pilot's War Memoirs or Regiments of the Burma Campaign*.

'Would you like to sit out on the patio?' The question was gently, even softly asked by his host.

They took their seats on canvas chairs which were placed side by side on the strip of red tiling, as if they were about to be photographed or to review a marching column. Tallboy moved his seat slightly out of symmetry so that he could see the three-quarter face of Jefferson. He consulted his notebook.

'How long did you know Reverend Gray, Mr Jefferson?'

Again, Jefferson appeared to be in no hurry to answer the question. He allowed his eyes to review the column of chrysanthemum seedlings in the pots arranged beside the small greenhouse. It was clear that the pace of the interview was going to be determined by this slow, strong man. Finally he said, 'Three years.'

‘So you knew him when he was a curate at Narborough?’

‘Quite right, Inspector.’ The tone was hard to interpret. Patronising? Sarcastic?

‘How did you first meet him?’

‘We shared,’ said Jefferson deliberately, ‘an interest in the morals of the younger generation. Youth work, Inspector, in a structured context.’

Tallboy was baffled. Where did Jefferson get phrases like ‘structured context’ from? ‘Isn’t that a young man’s field, Mr Jefferson? I always thought youth workers finished at thirty.’ Tallboy was jocose.

Jefferson didn’t bother to offer him any eye contact, let alone any response to his jocularity. ‘No,’ he said, ‘youth work has to be properly organised. Resources are necessary. You need leadership. That comes with experience.’ He swung round to look at Tallboy and raked him up and down with his eyes. ‘Fit leadership,’ he repeated as though the word ‘fit’ might not just be what the Medical Officer looked for. Tallboy shifted in his chair. It was a bit like listening to a sermon.

‘And you helped Paul Gray to provide that fit leadership?’

‘Yes. He needed help. He lacked organisation. And objectives. You’ve got to know what your objectives are.’

‘And what are your objectives in youth work, Mr Jefferson?’

‘Winnowing. Chaff from grain. Know what I mean, Inspector?’ His tone suggested that he did not pin much faith in this being the case. ‘You’ve got to face young lads with themselves. Help them to see what they’re made of. See if they can deal with their own fears and frailties, as it were. That’s the objective.’

Tallboy knew just enough of the probable training of youth workers to feel this might not be quite what the social studies lecturer had said. ‘You were in the services, were you, Mr Jefferson?’ he asked.

‘Twenty-two years in the Medewich Light Infantry.’

‘You can’t have been in the last war,’ said Tallboy invitingly.

'My privilege was Suez and Cyprus.'

Again Tallboy found it hard to judge the tone but if pressed he would have said it was sarky. 'A good thing, National Service, would you say, Mr Jefferson?' Tallboy asked apparently idly.

'Made men of some of those youngsters. Gave them a broader outlook, if you know what I mean. Gave them a chance to test themselves. Death as well as life. Not so different, a soldier's job, from the clergy when you think of it.'

'You've always been' — Tallboy wasn't sure how to phrase this one — 'interested in the Church have you?'

Jefferson allowed the words to hang in the air. 'Interested,' he said after a moment. 'Yes, that's about right. I've always been interested. We had some very good padres in the service. Men,' he said heavily, 'of integrity.' He stared at the chrysanthemums.

'And was Reverend Gray a man of integrity?'

There was a longish pause and then Jefferson said, 'Murder has to be punished. It's a matter of balance. Equal amounts of things. Every killed life by another killed life. We shouldn't stand in the way of the forces of justice, should we, Inspector?'

Tallboy himself was not without sympathy for this apocalyptic vision but it occurred to him to wonder who Jefferson thought the forces of justice were. 'So who murdered Paul Gray?'

'It's your job to find out, Inspector, and then see they're properly punished. Only you can't do that now, can you?'

'Do what?

'Punish them properly. Hang them by the neck until they're dead.'

The Inspector swallowed hard. 'Could we look at the night of the murder, last Thursday?' Tallboy consulted his notebook. 'It was Mr Gray's custom to pick you up from Medewich and take you out to Markham cum Cumbermound. Why was that? Don't you drive?'

'Yes, I drive all right but I prefer a motorbike. I can't carry equipment for a youth club on my bike, so Paul used to pick me up in his car.'

'Equipment?'

'Well, I service one or two youth clubs, particularly church clubs in the area and they share my equipment. Weights for lifting, bats and balls and that sort of thing. Sharing is a good use of resources.'

'So, you had the equipment assembled for Mr Gray on this particular evening, yes? But he didn't come?'

'Correct.'

'Could I look at the equipment?'

'What?' For the first time Jefferson appeared taken aback.

'Just routine.'

The ex-soldier rose easily from his chair and Tallboy followed him. In the corner of the living room behind them Jefferson indicated two boxes and a couple of canvas holdalls. Tallboy examined the mass of weights and balls. There was nothing odd in the stuff, as far as the Inspector could see. They returned to their seats on the patio.

'What time did Mr Gray usually pick you up?'

'About seven.'

'And what did you do when he didn't turn up on that Thursday?'

'I gave him half an hour and then I went for a spin.'

'Bike?'

'Motorbike.'

'Where?'

'Round and about.'

'Could you be more precise?'

'Round the bypass up to the airport. I had one or two acceleration problems I wanted to sort out.'

'He didn't ring you to cancel the club?'

'No.'

'Why didn't you ring Mrs Gray to find out where Paul had got to when he didn't turn up?'

There was a long pause. 'I got the impression Mrs Gray was not in favour of our work together.'

'Weren't you worried that he didn't turn up?'

'He wasn't always reliable. Like I told you, he wasn't organised. That's why he needed help.'

'Why didn't you go by bike to Markham cum Cumbermound's club?'

'I just said. You couldn't rely on him. If he'd cancelled the meeting, there'd be no point in me spending the petrol biking out there, would there? And without equipment too.'

'And you got back, you said in your first statement, at . . . ?'

'Ten o'clock, Inspector, just in time for the news and cocoa.' Tallboy was at a loss to know whether the big man was mocking him or not with these innocent tastes. I'll give him one more opening, he thought.

'Mr Jefferson, in your opinion, is there anyone who would have a reason to want to kill Mr Gray?'

'We've all got to die, Inspector.'

'He was twenty-nine.'

'I know lads who got theirs at eighteen in Cyprus.'

'But was there any particular person with a grudge against Mr Gray? Any of the parents of the Youth Club for example?'

The tall soldier smiled down at him. 'Let's just say we had a lot of satisfied customers amongst those young lads. Some of them were coming along fine. I know how to handle them. I've got the relevant experience, you see. And I care for them, of course.'

* * *

Mrs Thrigg plumped the coffee and home-made biscuits down on the low table beside the sofa in Mrs Baggley's drawing room and stumped out like a stage char. The Archdeacon's wife motioned to Theodora from her reclining position on her sofa by the window.

'Pour out, my dear, would you?'

Theodora did as she was asked.

'It is so good of you to look in on an old invalid when you must be so very busy at the office — what with the Dean's compost heap yielding such unwholesome remains.' Mrs Baggley was clearly avid for news.

Theodora had lodged in the attic flat of the Archdeaconry now for three years. It was a handsome building. She liked the Archdeacon, though she was slightly impatient of his apologetic manners. But she was aware that perhaps she underestimated his acceptability to the parochial clergy, who were not threatened by his gentleness. About his wife she had no reservations: tough and vital, the life force flowed through her even as the cancer — which she would acknowledge to no one, and certainly not to her husband — extended its grip on her. She listened now as Theodora retailed the to-ing and fro-ing of the clergy and police: the poor Dean, the remote Bishop, the worried Chief Constable, Mrs Gray.

'And the girl who seems to have the misfortune to be continually confronted by pieces of poor Paul Gray? How is she standing up to it all?'

Theodora considered. 'She's really doing rather well. She's both sensitive and tough. Oddly enough, I think her main troubles come rather more from not being English and not always being able to place people.'

'She finds the clergy a pain?' said Mrs Baggley acutely.

'Well, I think she finds the hierarchy surprising. Her instinct is to relate to everyone in the same way. She's truthful and spontaneous without being at all pushy or loud. But, of course, many clergy can't cope with that. They need reassurance, deference even.'

'Especially the ones higher up.'

'The senior clergy,' said Theodora quoting with a smile.

'So Charles bullies her?'

'I don't think he does in any special way. Just in the same way he bullies everyone below him. He tends to pick on new people a bit at first to bring them into line. Once they've made their submission he generally lets up.'

Mrs Baggley made a moue of distaste. 'Not my favourite gentleman,' she said. She drew her engagement ring down her fine finger and pushed it back again preparatory to making a move in a game. 'You know he was making rather a set at Paul Gray.'

Theodora noted the slang so typical of her mother's generation. 'Charles?' she responded. 'I rather gathered he might have been. Though since Gray was new in the diocese and a Bishop's favourite, I'm not surprised. Charles doesn't care for sibling rivals for the Bishop's favour.'

'You're a very noticing young woman,' said Mrs Baggley with affection. 'Yes, Bishop Thomas does rather proceed like King Lear at times, and of course it's tough on the family. I fear his son's death left an enormous gap. But I can't say I approve of his method of filling it. Having favourites turns the diocese into a Jacobean court — they all start plotting to do each other down.'

Theodora listened with interest to this colourful picture of the Bishop's managerial style.

'However,' Mrs Baggley resumed, 'I rather wonder whether Charles wasn't leaning very heavily indeed on Paul. I wonder if there wasn't something specific this time?'

Theodora looked alert and waited.

'You know Charles had Paul round several times recently, usually on Thursday evenings. In fact I rather gather he saw Paul the night he died.'

'Thursday evening? Do the police know?'

'I thought it best not to mention it,' said Mrs Baggley in a queenly fashion.

Theodora groaned inwardly.

'Of course, I see everything from my window.' Mrs Baggley was complacent. 'But I didn't actually see him myself on that particular evening. Mrs Thrigg' — Mrs Baggley had no shame in revealing her sources, all was grist to the mill. She leaned forward dramatically and her fine theatrical eye bore into Theodora — 'Mrs Thrigg did see him or at least heard him. She says there was a row. She happened to have dropped into Charles's to leave some shopping on her way over here. She says you could hear Canon Wheeler all down the stairs.'

'Saying what, exactly?' Theodora inquired with interest.

'Well, of course, Mrs Thrigg isn't much of a word-merchant so it's difficult to get anything exact out of her. She picks up tones and drifts rather than actual words. She says they were quarrelling over money and women.' Mrs Baggley examined the disbelief in Theodora's eye before she went on, 'I'm not sure how much Mrs Thrigg is influenced here by the theme of the novelettes she devours. She has a rather histrionic outlook on life sometimes. Is a little inclined to fantasise,' Mrs Baggley ended with a judicious air. Theodora hid her smile. 'But apparently,' Mrs Baggley returned to her previous committed tones, 'one phrase used by Canon Wheeler did strike her.' Mrs Baggley paused.

Come on, thought Theodora.

'Purity of motive.'

'Purity of motive, eh?' said Theodora.

'Quite so,' said Mrs Baggley impressively.

'Charles's or Gray's?'

'Presumably the latter if Charles was talking about them.'

'Well, he could have been defending his own,' Theodora said.

'Mrs Thrigg also said the Bishop was mentioned.'

'In what context?'

'Apparently Paul said something about he'd "like the Bishop to know".'

'Know what?'

'Something about his wife.'

Theodora's mind flashed back to the tall washed-out figure of Mrs Gray and her sudden passionate support of her husband's good intentions. 'No one more honourable, no one more truthful than Paul,' she had said. 'I don't care if he has a problem.' What had Wheeler got on Mrs Gray? Theodora wondered.

'What time did Paul get to Wheeler's? Does Mrs Thrigg know?'

'She arrived about seven thirty and they had had time enough to get to grips with their subject matter already, by all accounts.'

'What time did Gray leave Canon Wheeler's house?' She tried not to sound as though she were interrogating the older woman.

'That's all rather unfortunate,' said Mrs Baggley vexedly. 'Dick had a meeting with some Church Army people and I had to go and help with the coffee so I missed Paul coming out.'

Theodora sighed. She wondered whether to ask Mrs Baggley if she realised that she might have been the last person to see or hear of Paul Gray alive. Instead she said, 'I suppose Mrs Thrigg would have known when he left?'

Mrs Baggley snorted, 'No, she wouldn't. She came on here to help me with the coffee for the Church Army before Paul left.'

Theodora tried again, 'I suppose Paul came by car?'

'I haven't the least idea,' Mrs Baggley said loftily. 'If he did he'd have had to park at the back of St Manicus house since they've banned parking in the precinct now. Though what I did notice was a motorbike parked where it shouldn't have been — outside Wheeler's. Perhaps he came on that. Though come to think of it that's really rather unlikely because I'm almost certain I heard it rev up to depart very much later — sometime after midnight. I was sorry to miss him though. I might have had a word with him if I'd caught him. These Church Army people do talk so. It was well after nine by the time we got rid of them.'

'When you saw them off finally, did you notice anything else in the court?' Theodora had by now abandoned all attempts not to sound like an interrogator.

Mrs Baggley didn't seem to mind. She thought for a moment and then said, 'Well, actually I did see someone rather unexpected. I saw Geoffrey Markham — you know,

Cumbermound's youngest, coming from the direction of the Palace. I haven't seen him for simply ages, have you?'

'No,' said Theodora heavily. 'Are you sure?'

'Of course I'm sure,' said Mrs Baggley with impatience. 'I've known Geoffrey since he was at prep school. Rather a dangerous boy I always thought.'

'Mrs Baggley,' Theodora said earnestly, 'I do think it's awfully important to let the police have this information. If they're going to find out Paul Gray's killer they need to know as much as possible about his movements near to the time of his death.' She sought to convey the urgency of the situation. Up to now all had been surmise and suspicion. Mrs Baggley's evidence provided the first unshakeable facts about Paul's whereabouts after he had left his home on the evening of his murder.

Mrs Baggley looked sulky. 'I don't care for the notion that Paul Gray had his head cut off in the Cathedral. The whole idea is most unaesthetic. I'm sure he went away and had it done somewhere else. I think the old lunatic asylum would be a good place for it to have occurred, don't you?'

This is preposterous, thought Theodora. Murder wasn't a stage performance by the local thespians. They couldn't all just reject facts because they offended their sensibilities. She held her tongue, however, and tried another tack. 'Has Canon Wheeler told the police anything about his visits from Paul and his quarrel, would you suppose?'

'I really wouldn't know. I would hardly think so, would you? I mean it's not as though Charles actually cut Paul's head off. It just so happens that Paul had to make his visit there before going on to be decapitated somewhere else. I do think dirty linen should be kept in the family.'

Theodora felt the rare experience of anger. The clergy were going to make it impossible to find the young priest's murderer. She tried one last thrust. 'Wouldn't Mrs Thrigg have told the police about it?'

Mrs Baggley looked almost furtive. 'Well, of course Charles might not have known that Mrs Thrigg was actually in the house during the quarrel. And Mrs Thrigg does a number of our houses. She's been with us all for a long time. She and her crony Williams must be our longest serving Cathedral retainers. They make a very valuable team.' Mrs Baggley's pastoral tone was full of reproach at Theodora's lack of finer feeling in this area. 'We all know her, you see. It's quite natural she shouldn't want to tattle to the police, isn't it?'

'Oh, quite,' said Theodora in despair. There were no cracks anywhere. Naturally, Mrs Thrigg might not want to lose half a dozen agreeable jobs. And if they all spied on each other all the time the great thing, the only thing, which would, could, make life tolerable was to pretend that they didn't. It looked as though she'd have to have a word with Mrs Thrigg.

'That secretary of his,' said Mrs Baggley with an inconsequence which was only apparent, 'feeds Charles with far too much tittle-tattle. What's her name? Coldharbour, yes, Rosamund Coldharbour. She, of course, knew Paul in his first parish at St Simeon's at Narborough. I think she still lives in the parish and commutes in. She knew a bit too much about Paul's distressing business with his youth club there.'

Theodora kept her eyes down. It was clear Mrs Baggley was, in her own way, making comments about a possible motive for Gray's murder. If Mrs Baggley wanted to talk this one out Theodora would listen but she had no intention of inviting anything that might be just gossip. On the other hand, she reflected, it would fit well with all that she knew of Miss Coldharbour's habits if she had fed Wheeler with information about Gray which he'd used to bully Gray with. She remembered the list of names in *Crockford* which Julia had come upon.

Once launched, moreover, Mrs Baggley was not going to be denied her hypothesising. 'You know there was absolutely nothing pinned on Paul at Narborough. My information was that the real cause of the trouble there was a man called Jefferson. Some sort of ex-military man who'd been having some rather rough games with some of the boys. Once Paul realised what was going on he'd put a stop to it. His only stupidity was that he was a bit slow about picking up what was actually happening. But that he did, or wanted to do, anything discreditable is quite untrue. Dick felt quite sure about that.'

'I know nothing came to court,' said Theodora. 'The Bishop and your husband supported Paul.'

'I should think so indeed,' said Mrs Baggley. 'Privilege has its obligations.'

'His wife,' Theodora said hesitantly, 'Mrs Gray, did suggest to me that he had a problem.'

'If you mean he liked men as well as women, I think that may well have been true,' said Mrs Baggley robustly. 'It's not his sexual propensities that matter. Many men like both sexes. Women too, I expect. It's what he chooses to do about that liking which matters. Personally, I think that in choosing to wed a nice girl like Eunice Gray and have a son he made a very sensible move. I really can't believe ill of him. On the two occasions he came here, I thought him a charming youth. Sincere, honest, humorous. I hate to think of him dead and in so horrid a way.'

'Yes,' said Theodora and thought of Julia.

* * *

Julia, in the cubby-hole of her office, ticked the last item on Miss Coldharbour's list, 'Agenda for Chapter Meeting'. She drew breath for the first time in three and a quarter hours. Her neck ached with tension. She was about to risk departing for an early lunch, a move which she would not have dared to make if Miss Coldharbour had been in the office, but Julia gathered she was out for the morning and not expected in until two fifteen. Mary, at reception, had given her this useful piece of information after taking Miss Coldharbour's call.

Julia was all the more dismayed, therefore, as she leaned back in her chair, to hear the unmistakable tread of Canon Wheeler coming down the corridor. She was partly at a loss to account for her fear of the man, which was surely irrational. Even granted he had the power to sack her, that would not be the end of the world. Tenuous as her typing talents were, she was certain she could market them elsewhere. Of Canon Wheeler's moral superiority to herself she was unconvinced. Why, then, did she find herself shaking and hoping that the tread would continue past her door?

The door swung open and Canon Wheeler's tall and immaculately tailored presence filled the space. She rose unconfidently to her feet. He surveyed her for a moment and then switched on, as though it had been a light, the very considerable charm of his smile.

'Do you think you could possibly look in on me in about fifteen minutes? I've got a couple of letters I'd like to get off before lunch.'

'Yes, sir,' said Julia, resisting his charm with all her suspicious heart.

She found herself running a comb through her hair, taking a shorthand pad and three pencils instead of the two which should surely have been enough, running a handkerchief over her dusty sandals and easing her left-hand stocking round her ankle a bit to keep the ladder out of sight. This was ludicrous. She found her hands were sweating. Fifteen minutes. That gave her time to go for a quick wash. She shot out of the office and down the stairs. Damnation, Miss Coldharbour was coming up. They met halfway. She murmured a 'good morning' and did not ask her what the hell she was doing there so unexpectedly.

'Were you going out?' inquired Miss Coldharbour with her customary detachment, as though it were in Julia's power to determine her hours of work.

'Canon Wheeler wants some dictation. I was just going for a wash,' said Julia who was well aware that Miss Coldharbour would make the connection between those two statements.

'Ah, yes,' said Miss Coldharbour lightly. Her handsome features betrayed no emotion as Julia stood aside to give her passage.

A sudden curiosity swept over Julia, coupled with a wish to disturb that perfect demeanour. 'Is Canon Wheeler married?' she asked.

‘I beg your pardon?’ Miss Coldharbour stopped in her tracks one step above Julia. She did not turn round to utter her question.

‘I wondered if Canon Wheeler had a wife?’ repeated Julia.

‘No.’ Miss Coldharbour’s monosyllable perfectly conveyed that Julia’s question was impertinent.

Just as well, thought Julia as she continued downstairs, poor hypothetical woman.

Exactly fifteen minutes later, Julia tapped once on the panelled door of the double cube, paused, turned the handle and entered. The form of Canon Wheeler could be seen in his chair below the Masaccio copy. Julia, who when nervous found it difficult to see things clearly, started the long haul down the lilac carpet. She took her stand in front of the desk. Wheeler did not move. Steadying her breathing, Julia focused on his powerful figure. His head, she realised was at an odd angle. His slightly protuberant eyes, she saw, were not moving. After a moment or two she reached for the telephone and contacted the police.

Then she rang Theodora, who rang Ian.

CHAPTER NINE: EARTH HAS GOT ON EARTH A DIGNITY OF NAUGHT

The Cathedral clock rang out the three-quarter: fifteen minutes before midnight. Caretaker yawned. He longed to smoke but dared not. If nothing happened by two o'clock he'd abandon his vigil and let the police know about the car number plate and, of course, the candles. He shifted in his chair and looked out of the window. There was a full moon over the Cathedral. Canon Hardnut's first-floor front drawing room, next door to Canon Wheeler's on one side and Canon Sylvester's on the other, gave an excellent view of the south door and the St Manicus chapel. It was not, however, with this that Ian's interest lay.

He went again over the row he'd had that morning with Wheeler. He flushed with anger at the things Wheeler had said to him, even though he knew they weren't true. Wheeler had faced it out, just as he had feared he might, denied everything, appeared not to understand the evidence and ended the interview by thumping the table and telling him he could expect his dismissal in writing before the end of the month. Ian, fortified to some degree by his small new knowledge and large new guesses about Wheeler's conduct, had found himself sufficiently detached to watch the canon's physiological symptoms of anger, wondering why he had never attended to them before. Wheeler's fair complexion had flushed, the pale-grey eyes bulged, his breathing rate went up and a line of spittle had formed on his lower lip. How much did Wheeler believe himself, act himself into believing himself? How much, Ian had wondered, was he self-deceiving and how much just a normal frightened liar? There was a side to the clerical role which demanded powers of acting: perhaps Wheeler could no longer draw the line.

Once freed from his presence, however, the psychology of Wheeler had ceased to detain Ian. He had formed his resolution and clattered down the front staircase to the office of the absent diocesan secretary, intent on following the one lead which, if it held, would undoubtedly shop Wheeler.

An hour later Theodora had telephoned him to announce Wheeler's death. They had met, the three of them — Julia, Theodora and Ian — in the latters' attic office. There they had pooled their information. Ian had told Theodora about finding Paul's number plates at Cumbermound and had gone on to tell them both something of what he had learned from Miss Coldharbour later that same evening after the Medewich show. Theodora had repeated what Mrs Baggley had told her about Paul's visit to Wheeler and the conversation Mrs Thrigg had overheard. The decisive point in crystallizing Ian's thinking had been Mrs Baggley's remark about her having seen Markham in Canons' Court on Thursday evening. The connections which had been shaping themselves in Ian's head had suddenly seemed to make sense.

The rest had been pure agony for someone of Ian's impatient temperament. First Julia had been called for questioning, then he himself had had to go in. It was not until after lunch when, evading the kind invitation of the two women to join them for food, he'd mumbled something about testing theories and made his way back to the wherry. There was no point in alarming them and anyway he might be wrong. He'd shot out of the office, stopping only to pick up the St Saviour's candle from Theodora's desk. Once back at the wherry he'd taken the asylum candle from its resting place in the press beneath his bunk and, knowing now what to look for, had no difficulty in spotting the dark circle in its base which formed a plug to a cavity large enough to conceal a small packet. Holding his breath he had gently eased a knife round the mark. The amazing thing was that it was full. He repeated the experiment with the St Saviour's candle but this one, though it had the same cavity, was empty. He was finally convinced there could be no doubt about what was happening.

The next step had been more difficult. There was really only the presence of Markham in the court that Thursday evening to go on. But having discovered the contents of the candles, Ian was sure that his earlier theory that money was the link between Gray and Markham was correct. And he was sure now that Gray had met his end somewhere in the court. The only question was where? There were two houses empty, the deceased Hardnut's and that of Sylvester, who was on sabbatical. It would be only sensible to suppose that anyone looking for a repository for the candles would use the house of the deceased rather than the merely absent canon. And if the street value of the stuff in the candles was anything to go by they'd be back to claim it. What had happened, he wondered, to let two such valuable vessels loose in such diverse contexts? Some breakdown in the ordinance. Anyway it provided a motive for murder. If Gray had been part of that sort of game, or if he'd stumbled on it and threatened to reveal all, Markham would have had quite strong reasons for killing him. And if Wheeler had observed some of Markham's comings and goings from his cottage on the Cumbermound estate, or indeed in the court itself, that might be a reason for Markham's appearing on his hit list.

So, weighing the possibilities, Caretaker had come to Canon Hardnut's as soon as he could be sure that the police had finished with him. It had been about seven in the evening. He'd not been eager for anyone to see him enter, so he'd come in through the back, alert to every trace on the way, sure now of what he was looking for. He'd had the spare keys, of course, to Canon Hardnut's. They'd been lying there on Williams's keyboard just as he'd seen them when he'd spoken to Williams. Once inside the house he'd inspected every inch of the ground. There was not too much to see. The police, if they had searched the house (and Ian could imagine the Dean, with his strong sense of decorum, might not have been eager to give approval for too much disturbance of the relicts of the deceased Canon) might be forgiven for not finding anything especially if, unlike Ian, they had not been specifically directed there. He had found a smudge of fresh tar on the door mat and a single small dark blot at the foot of the staircase.

In an effort to turn his thoughts away from the horror, Ian put his hand in his pocket and fingered the stump of candle with the St Manicus arms on it, wondering what to do with such an incriminating object. After some deliberation he'd kept the asylum one on his own person and sent the one Theodora had given him to Julia at her lodgings by special messenger, with instructions attached. Then, when he'd entered Canon Hardnut's study he'd searched high and low for others. He'd found one very well concealed in the elephant-foot umbrella stand, a piece of stage scenery which accurately represented the style of Canon Hardnut's life. The only question was, was this all there was or were there more? And, having thought about it, he'd based his long vigil on the idea that one was enough but there might be others. And, with this latest death, whoever had secreted the candles would know another search could be imminent, and so they'd be likely to return to make sure it wasn't fruitful. Ian would soon know if he was right.

As he stared into the gloom he thought how the sacrilege would have appealed to Geoffrey. The top of the candle burning on the altar to symbolise the illumination afforded the world by the Christian gospel and the hidden base concealing that element which could most easily destroy a man. It was the same cast of mind which would not merely have killed someone but severed his head and put it in a font and then replaced the weapon in its ceremonial position. How very typical of Geoffrey.

He recalled him at Cambridge. Small, dark, impish or devilish, according to whether one loved or hated him. He had spent a lot of his time mixing with actors and producing the odd play, Ian remembered. Not unlike his father in figure, his tone and accent he had modified in the modern manner to imitate the fashionable glottal stop. He'd enjoyed being the reputed Geoffrey Markham, Cumbermound's son, who speaks like a navvy. He was attractive enough, to both men and women and quite unscrupulous in using both to further his ends, although sexually he'd stuck to the latter. The last occasion he'd seen him in Cambridge had been at the party which had ended with Thomas Newcome's death. Suicide, perhaps, or perhaps not. Ian had retained the memory of Geoffrey's face bending over the pale features of the Bishop's son as he lay on the bed with the lethal mixture of alcohol and drugs inside him. Geoffrey's own features had registered something which, on reflection, Ian could only interpret as triumph, even glee. He'd put his arm round Ian's shoulder and drawn him down to look at the dead boy. He had put his finger to his lips and said, 'Look, Ian, our brother doth but sleep.'

Ian felt his stomach heave at the memory. Could he have saved Thomas? he wondered. What sort of perversity inspired Geoffrey? At that moment, certainly, he'd seen him as devilish. He'd known him a long time. They'd been at the same prep school. In those days he'd shown a talent for making the lives of certain sorts of fellow pupil hellish. The characters he'd particularly been drawn to were very straightforward, unsuspecting boys. His ploy was to befriend them, lead them into some sort of scrape and then betray them to the authorities. He liked, he really loved, he'd once boasted, to see the look of bewilderment on their faces when they realised what had been done to them. 'I have a very important place in the scheme of things,' he'd said once. 'I'm here to show them the roaring lion seeking whom he may devour. In other words, what the world is really like.'

Was that what he'd done to Thomas? He'd known Thomas was taking drugs at school and in quite heavy quantities. He suspected his father, the Bishop, did not know. There was no confidence between the Bishop and his son. The sensible thing for Ian to have done would have been to tell the Bishop. The plain fact was, however, that Ian had been afraid to do that. Afraid for himself, irrationally, but afraid also for Thomas, perhaps with more reason. The Bishop was, after all, formidable. And because of that quality, the quality which prevented people from facing him, the Bishop had lost his son. My fault, wondered Ian, my most grievous fault? Or his?

Three years later, Ian remembered, he and Geoffrey had met again in London. He'd suspected that Geoffrey was pushing drugs. He couldn't quite believe that anyone he knew would actually do that. But the memory of Thomas's face as he lay dying and of Geoffrey's glee had haunted him. There'd been a fight at that London party. Ian remembered what he'd said to Geoffrey, words which had caused Geoffrey to throw his wine in Ian's face and had resulted in Ian hitting him hard enough on the side of the head to knock him down. Oddly enough, Ian thought with surprise, what he'd read on Geoffrey's face as he lay on the floor, was that same look of gleeful triumph he'd had when he'd viewed Thomas's body, almost as though he'd successfully achieved what he wanted. But Ian had had no regrets about the blow. It wouldn't restore young Thomas but it had been some sort of just retribution.

Ian stirred as the clock struck the hour. Midnight. If his intuition was right and if the various bits of the puzzle which he'd been manoeuvring every which way over the past forty-eight hours were correct, Geoffrey would surely make some attempt to clear the scene of evidence — quite apart from the monetary aspect involved. Then, thought Ian grimly, he could clear one or two things out of the way before letting the police in.

Ian leant his forehead against the cool pane of the window to keep himself awake. In the remains of the moonlight he remarked a slim, black cat emerge from Canon Wheeler's garden. With elaborate theatricality, freezing every five yards and then streaking forward, it gained the top of the garden wall. There it stopped suddenly and swished its tail once. Ian looked to see the cause of its immobility. At the other end of the wall, with its back to the black cat but nevertheless managing to convey that it perceived its presence, was a heftier, long-haired version. Ian was about to immerse himself in what he knew might be a prolonged, silent contest of wills, when, without warning, both cats plopped down from the wall and shot off in different directions. Ian peered about to see what had disturbed them. From round the corner of the Cathedral, a figure could be seen making its way towards the entrance to the St Manicus chapel.

Ian held his breath and then let it out again. It was the figure of a woman. Damnation. No woman had entered his calculation with regard to Geoffrey and his outfit. He felt unreasonable resentment that he was to be confronted with some new piece of the game at this juncture. Moreover the woman was making for the St Manicus chapel entrance. On Ian's reckoning she, or better he, should have been entering Canon Hardnut's front or back door. However, anyone entering the St Manicus chapel at midnight, apparently with their own key, could not be your normal tourist. Ian wondered whether the police might have left anyone on guard in the Cathedral. He rather thought not. There really could be no reason for doing so and he expected they were undermanned.

He picked up his jacket from beside his chair and moved quickly and quietly down the elegant stairs. In the hall he paused. If he made for the back door he'd lose minutes while he went round the back of Canons' Court. If he let himself out through the front door, he might be seen. He chanced it. The large, well-balanced door opened silently and he slipped through and down the garden path to the iron gate at the end. The gate had been oiled recently and gave no sound.

Ian sprinted across to the St Manicus chapel door. Cautiously he felt the cold iron handle. He turned it experimentally. It did not open. He had no Cathedral keys with him: he had not expected any business there. What now? He could, of course, wait until whoever it was came out and collar them then. But since whoever it was appeared to have a key to the St Manicus chapel, why shouldn't they have keys to the other doors? They might exit by any one of them. Including, thought Ian, the joker in the pack: the Bishop's door. But if she, why not he? Ian turned swiftly towards the east end, rounded the apse and arrived at the north side beside the small undecorated stonework of the Bishop's door. He tried the latch both ways. No movement. Good for his lordship, or rather, on this occasion, bad for his lordship. Ian thought again. He'd try the Vergers' entrance on the north side on the off chance. If that wasn't open he'd take his station again by the St Manicus chapel entrance and hope.

The Vergers' entrance, with its clutter of mops and washing line, was darker than the other side. Cautiously, Ian decided to use his torch. His neat, powerful rubber flashlight showed him his path between the detritus. Down two steps to the first door. He tried the handle. It opened easily. Lazy, careless bastards. The passage smelt stale and dusty. He pressed on towards the second door which led into the crypt vestry office. It occurred to him that even if he gained the crypt, the door from the crypt to the Cathedral might well, jolly well ought to, be locked. Sufficient unto the day, however. He tried the second door. It too opened easily. Ian pointed the flashlight round the room. His eye was caught by an object on the table next to the inevitable copy of *The Sun*. He crossed to examine it. He took the object gingerly in his hand. It was familiar to him. A whetstone, used by carpenters for sharpening chisels or knives or swords. It had recently been oiled and so was in use. Ian wondered, given this latest discovery, whether he really wanted to proceed to the body of the Cathedral.

While he was hesitating, he heard a slight noise apparently from overhead. Ian stepped swiftly through the office door, out into the crypt. He thought of First World War troops taught to shout as they charged with fixed bayonets towards other human beings. He thought of Dhani, 'breathe it out, shout it out.' He allowed all his own anger at the murder and mutilation of a young man and the desecration of places of worship to flow through him and leapt from the crypt stairs and through the door. It hardly surprised him that it was open. The crypt entrance into the Cathedral emerged beside the choir screen and the organ loft. He made for the central entrance to the choir through the door behind the nave altar. He had pocketed his torch and relied on the light of the building but as he came through the choir entrance, he saw that there were lights kindled.

Twenty yards away from him and directly in front of the high altar were two candles held aloft by human hands. He could just make out a small huddle of people in a circle. As he raced towards them, there was an appalling sound midway between a scream and a crow. Ian bellowed his own battle cry at the group as he launched himself towards one of the candle-holding hands. A woman's voice shrieked and a man's could be heard shouting, 'Out, out'.

Ian held on to the hand and one of the candles rolled away and extinguished itself on the stone floor. The other candle the man forced into Ian's face making him shout with pain as it burnt his cheek. With more presence of mind than he would have credited himself he held on to the man and blew out the candle. In utter darkness they continued to wrestle together, the thought of how ill-trained he was flashing helplessly through Ian's mind. All he'd ever undergone had been a modest programme of martial arts with Dhani, designed far more to help him release aggression than actually capture or hurt anyone.

The figure broke away from him and shot off down the choir aisle towards the nave. The one physical pursuit which Ian had any skill in was rugby and his schoolboy instincts didn't fail him now. He lunged forward in an excellent imitation of an under-fifteen eager to secure his place in the team and was rewarded by a pleasing thud as the other hit the ground. But he too appeared to have the rudiments of the game at his command. He struggled manfully to his feet with Ian still hanging on to his knees and then kicked back into his face. Ian tasted the blood in his mouth and atavistic anger coursed through him. He had more weight than the other man. He heaved himself up the other's body and leant his knee into the small of the man's back. Then he crooked his left arm round the man's neck, wrenched it back and then knocked it forward again on to the stone floor. There was a choking gasp and the man went limp. Ian took his knee out of the man's back and rolled him over. He took out his flash-light and allowed it to play over the recumbent form. The man's head was encased in a hood which had partly come off. Ian jerked at it and surveyed the familiar face beneath.

'You Welsh bastards always did play a dirty game,' he murmured.

* * *

Julia found the parcel with Ian's neat handwriting on it on the floor of the entrance hall when she returned to her attic lodgings at about quarter to twelve. The protracted police questioning had exhausted her utterly. They'd called her back for a second go about six o'clock. After that, in the absence of Theodora who had an engagement at a training session out in the fens, she'd lingered over a sandwich at the 'Adam and Eve' on the waterfront before walking up through the town to her lodgings. But when she saw the clear hand on the re-used brown paper her energy returned. She took up the note propped against it.

J: Here is the number plate and Theodora's candle. If I'm not back in the office by 9 a.m. tomorrow take them to the police and suggest they talk to Geoffrey Markham. Get them to look at the base and analyse chemically any traces they find there. Don't be frightened.
Bless you, I. H. C.

Julia stared at the parcel. She began to be frightened. What was Ian going to do? He'd not revealed his intentions to her and Theodora when they had met earlier that day, before the police moved in. The last she had seen of him was when he'd shot off, murmuring something about testing theories. For a moment it had looked as though Theodora had wanted to stop him but in the end she'd said nothing. The parcel had the stamp 'Hermes' on its back, the device of the local special messengers sometimes used by the diocesan office. She had no idea how long it had been there. Where was Ian? Had he then gone on to confront Markham? What exactly was Markham's connection with her cousin's murder? The little Ian had told them about Markham had convinced her that he was a dangerous man. Was he capable of murder? And had he killed not only Paul but Canon Wheeler as well? And if so, why? She took the parcel and extracted the candlestick. On its base was the familiar pattern of the St Manicus arms. She turned it up and looked closely at its base. There was a sort of plug in it which her fingers couldn't shift. Chemical analysis, had Ian written?

Even as her fear mounted, she heard, two storeys below her, the sound of a fist pounding on the front door of the house. If her landlord, Mr Docherty, was out, as he currently appeared to be, her usual way of dealing with callers was to open the casement window and lean out. It was much too dark to follow this course now. The banging came again, aggressive and prolonged. Such knocking so late re-echoing through the empty house terrified her. On an impulse she gathered up Ian's note and the parcel and slipped them into the pocket of her Barbour. She grabbed her purse and pushed it into her cords' pocket and hurried downstairs.

As she reached the ground floor, she heard someone trying the front door. She stepped swiftly forward and as quietly as possible shot the bolt beneath the latch. Then she turned and fled downstairs to the basement kitchen, quietly opened the back door and hurried out into the overgrown back garden. Two ancient pear trees overshadowed it, making it darker than the large full moon warranted. The long, matted grass of the lawn concealed many hazards: ancient sinks and the forgotten parts of a children's tricycle. Once in the open, however, Julia felt calmer. She made her way to the end of the garden and wrestled with the rotten garden gate. A moment or two later, she got it open far enough to allow her to squeeze through into the lane which ran the length of the backs of the two rows of terrace houses.

She unhooked her jacket from the rusty catch and started off down the hill towards the end of the lane which ran into the main road a hundred yards away. She glanced down and thought she caught sight of a bulky figure just appearing at the end. Without hesitation she swung off in the opposite direction which was in fact the shorter way but was uphill. Before she reached the end of the lane she heard the sound of running feet. Without looking back she broke into a run. She was fast and she ran at full speed, making no attempt to disguise the fact that she was running away. She rounded the end of the lane and plunged into the main road. There were two or three people in sight but none near at hand. What there was, however, was a bus just gliding up to the stop twenty yards down the road. Julia spurted towards it and swung herself through the closing door. Once inside she looked back. There still appeared to be about the same number of people in the road. It was difficult to tell if the man in the army surplus flak jacket caught in the light of a street lamp had been there all the time or whether he had just emerged from the end of the lane.

Gratefully she fumbled for a fare and panted her way to a back seat. Once flopped down on the bench, she reviewed her position. The sensible thing, surely, would be to go to the police with her parcel now and tell them all she knew about Ian and the car number plate and the candle. But, first, she didn't know very much and second, she might be endangering Ian. She shrank too from informing the police about anything which might reflect discreditably on her cousin. She wished fervently she believed in prayer, that she knew how to pray. She thought of Theodora and the thought brought relief. She knew that Theodora had rooms in the Archdeaconry. She knew she kept late hours. She longed for her steady, sane presence. Might it not be worth dropping in there and, if there was no joy there, going across to the *Amy Roy?*

Having made this resolution, Julia felt calmer. At the bottom of Market Street she got off the bus and walked through the market square. She paused at the butter cross and looked back. Just parking a powerful looking motorbike on the park the other side of the square was a man in a combat jacket. Julia had no idea if it was the same man she had seen half a mile away or whether he was following her and if so whether his intent was hostile or not. But she felt her breathing becoming faster again and broke into a brisk walk in the direction of the Archdeaconry to the south of the Cathedral. There were still a few people about, tourists and townspeople, near the west door, but as she made her way round Canons' Court, they lessened in number. Julia glanced back over her shoulder. There was no sign of flak-jacket.

She swung open the iron gate to the short stone path to the front door and hastened up the front steps. She pressed the old-fashioned, beautifully cleaned brass bell stop on the door case and waited. Midnight. She pressed again. Surely they couldn't both be out. Then she remembered Theodora had told her that her flat was entered by an iron staircase at the back of the Archdeaconry. Julia peered back into Canons' Court. She could not be sure but she thought she saw the figure of a man rounding the south door by St Manicus chapel. She slipped down the narrow gravel passage at the side of the house which separated the Archdeaconry from Canons' Court and made her way via the dustbins to the rear of the house. With relief she started up the iron staircase. Julia could just make out a bell with Theodora's name under it. She pushed it and tried the door handle. The door, a modern affair of flimsy wood with glass panels in it, opened easily inward and Julia stumbled inside.

Then she stopped. The room, clearly a sitting room, was a shambles. Books had been thrown off the shelves, rugs pulled up. Drawers in the dresser lay open and in turmoil. Of Theodora there was no sign. Once again Julia felt panic rising in her. Clearly someone had been here looking for something. Was it candles or number plates or something else?

Julia turned to look back at the door through which she had just entered. She closed it behind her and pushed the bolt to. Then she moved quietly through to the landing. She listened intently. There was no sound. Then she thought she detected a crunch of gravel. Swiftly she descended the staircase which changed from the utilitarian one up to Theodora's flat into the much grander one leading into the main body of the house. Very little moonlight came through the lantern above her or from the fanlight over the front door below her. She felt trapped in an encroaching gloom. She didn't think there was anyone at home. She crossed the stone-flagged floor of the Archdeaconry hall and stood listening at the front door. Then she turned the handle, opened it a crack and looked towards the iron gate through which she had passed a few minutes ago. She had closed it. Now it stood open.

Julia ceased to hesitate. She flung herself down the path and out through the gate. Instead of turning left, back the way she had come in the direction of the market square and the west end of the Cathedral, she turned right and pelted down towards the footbridge; a quicker way over the river to the *Amy Roy* but, she realised as she ran, one which was much less frequented.

In the increasing darkness, Julia hurtled towards the bridge, the heavy car number plate in her Barbour pocket flapping clumsily against her ribs. As she neared the bridge, she looked back and saw flak-jacket sprinting in a business-like manner down the length of Canons' Court. She'd made a mistake. She should never have come this way. Panting now with panic as much as physical effort, Julia cleared the bridge, turned right along the tow path and leaped down on to the deck of the *Amy Roy*.

'Dhani?' she gasped. 'Dhani, where are you?'

There was no reply. Julia had a vision of herself floating downstream with her neck at an odd angle. She looked back along the tow path. Flak-jacket had not yet appeared. She made her way aft.

Dhani appeared up the companion way. He looked at Julia.

'What is it?' he asked in a low steady voice.

'Oh, Dhani, thank God.'

Dhani took her hand in both of his and drew her down into the cabin. Before she could sit down, however, there was a clatter and the wherry jerked at her moorings.

'Dhani,' Julia found herself whispering, 'it's them. It's Paul's killers. I'm certain of it. I don't know who they are or why they did it but I'm sure it's them.'

Dhani replied by putting his finger to his lips and motioning her to move down the cabin. Then he stationed himself on the other side nearer the door. The cabin was almost dark and the moonlight outside practically gone.

Julia had never seen anything like it. From the minute he burst through the door, it was clear the figure in the flak-jacket knew all about combat techniques. On the other hand Dhani had spent four hours a day for five years practising martial arts. It was quite clear to her that flak-jacket intended to kill Dhani and that he was much heavier and more powerful than him. On the other hand Dhani gave a feeling of a kind of dancing vitality, almost of enjoyment. In another context he would have been beautiful to watch. If he killed, thought Julia, rigid with horror, it would be beautifully, ritually, like a ballet. But she didn't think Dhani was out to kill. Pressed against the wooden sides of the cabin she watched him use every part of his body in complete harmony, employing every inch of the confined space. Flak-jacket would have done better, thought Julia in a moment of detached appraisal, if he'd had more room: though he looked lethal, really his style was based on boxing or at most wrestling, so it was well suited for attack and for opponents who resisted him. Dhani, on the other hand, never made an aggressive move. His style was based on evasion and on letting the heavier man exhaust himself. Time after time, what looked like a movement which would result in his being cornered and destroyed ended in the heavier man frustrated and wrong-footed. And finally, youth and technique prevailed. The big man, less nimble than Dhani, missed his footing, Dhani chopped neatly downwards on the back of his neck with his left hand and the man slumped to the ground.

Dhani stood panting slightly, the pupils of his eyes, Julia noticed, dilated like an animal's. For a moment he looked almost unrecognisable. As the tension of her fear unwound itself it flashed across her mind to wonder whether he had used his physical skill in another context recently. Suddenly there was sound of voices on the deck above.

'Hello,' said an English voice. 'Anyone there? Everything all right?'

Dhani didn't reply for a moment. Then he lifted his head. Two inquiring faces could just be made out peering down the companionway.

'Yes,' said Dhani. 'All right now, come down.'

There was a clatter of footsteps as two men descended. They seemed immediately to take possession of the situation. One addressed a remark in Dutch to the other and pointed to the recumbent body of flak-jacket. He turned him over with his foot and exclaimed. The other man bent to look closer, then he straightened up. He put his right hand in the pocket of his trousers and smiled at Julia.

'We've come over from the boat next door,' he said. 'We thought we heard voices. My name, by the way, is Geoffrey Markham.'

* * *

At two in the morning Ian had rung the police from the Archdeaconry. The Archdeacon had agreed that there was no hope of keeping the desecration quiet. He'd rung the

Bishop and got no answer; so he'd rung the Dean and they'd agreed to call the police. Williams was under arrest on the rather dubious charge of trespass on Church property until the lawyers could look up something suitably esoteric about sacrilege.

The Archdeacon and Mrs Baggley had been kindness itself to Ian. He had pounded on their door at one o'clock and collapsed through it when the Archdeacon, muffled in a threadbare towelling robe and but lately returned with his wife from an engagement in Narborough, had at last opened it. Mrs Baggley had appeared seconds later at the top of the stairs dramatically swathed in a purple and green watered silk peignoir. Her splendid array had not prevented her being extremely efficient with hot water, lint and whisky for Ian. Theodora, clad in a green tartan dressing gown that looked as though it might be bulletproof, had assisted unflappably.

Mrs Baggley had enjoyed herself hugely. It was the second disturbance they had had that evening. Theodora, returning at a little after midnight from a confirmation training, had been unable to get into her flat, finding the door bolted against her. When she had come up through the main entrance she had found the place in disarray. At first she had thought of not mentioning it or making a fuss. Nothing had been taken as far as she could tell. Then she remembered Paul Gray and Canon Wheeler and had asked the Archdeacon to get the police. Almost at once two tired-looking men in a squad car had appeared and spent ten minutes making nothing of it. They had advised her not to touch anything and promised to return in the morning when they could find a man to deal with the fingerprints, if there were any. Theodora wondered whether they were inefficient or short of manpower and bedded down in the Archdeacon's spare room for the night. Fifteen minutes later they had all risen to welcome Ian.

When the police had arrived, the Archdeacon, Ian and the Dean had accompanied them to the Cathedral to pick up Williams whom Ian had locked in the vestry office. He was only just coming to, Ian noticed with satisfaction and was clearly in great pain. The police had hustled him out and taken the candles and the pathetic body of a cockerel with them.

The Dean had looked mournfully at the high altar and murmured about holy water and reconsecration. Really, Ian had thought for a moment, there is no difference between us and them: devil worshippers use blood, the Church water. But he looked at the Archdeacon's tired face and remembered Mrs Baggley's kindness and acquitted them of magic practices.

Afterwards, the three of them with Theodora and Mrs Baggley sipped whisky in the Archdeacon's under-furnished library. The caryatids supporting the fireplace gazed back at them noncommittally. Too many paperbacks, thought Ian, snobbishly reviewing the Archdeacon's book stock, but there was nothing wrong with the single malt.

'I'm so glad,' said the Archdeacon as he raised his eyes from the heavy glass tumbler and gazed at the younger man. 'I'm so enormously grateful to you. It's a tremendous weight off my mind. You've no idea. I knew, that is, I felt something was amiss. You know how one does.'

'In that case,' said the Dean severely, 'why didn't you tell me?'

'I was afraid, I suppose, to voice my fears. What if I were wrong? What if I were fanciful? It is fantastic. It seems to reflect on one's sanity. But actually, I've had a series of phone calls recently which were very disturbing and which I suppose may have been connected with this business. I really blame myself for not doing something about them.'

'What sort of calls?' asked the Dean.

'All very odd and all the same. I suppose they were a sort of curse.'

'What sort of curse?'

'Well, there you have it. They simply cursed me. Not casually, you understand, as people sometimes do in ordinary speech. But ritually, if you get my meaning, as though they really wanted my death or damnation. I think it may, on reflection, have been a woman's voice.'

Mrs Baggley put out her hand. 'Dick, love, I wish you'd told me.'

'I didn't want to worry you,' said the Archdeacon apologetically.

'Had the Bishop any inkling?' asked the Dean.

'I rather think he may have done. I've remarked his walking at night in the environs of the Cathedral over the past year or so. Of course there is no reason why he shouldn't use the Cathedral for prayer or meditation. Though he has his private chapel in the Palace.'

'He never mentioned anything to you?'

'No. I wonder if he didn't mention it to me for the same reason I didn't mention it to him.'

'You mean, out of fear,' said the Dean thoughtfully. 'He's been frightened about his mental health since his wife died and that business about his son which,' he glanced at Ian, 'I gather you know something about.'

Ian flushed and moved uncomfortably in his chair.

'He feared madness perhaps,' said Theodora. 'Like Lear?' she added, glancing at Mrs Baggley.

'I think perhaps,' said the Dean, 'he began to mistrust his own judgement and for that reason has withdrawn from the business of the diocese. I think too, that about the use of the Cathedral, he may not have been able to be quite straightforward. You see, I happen to know that Williams supplies him with some sort of homeopathic medicine for his arthritis. There is no reason to suppose the Bishop couldn't have got adequate drugs from a regular doctor or have gone on his own account to a homeopath if he'd wanted. But the medicine Williams supplied him with seemed to work and he'd come to rely on it. I think he couldn't, for that reason, bear either to change or to look too closely into Cathedral matters for fear of what he should find out about Williams.'

There was silence as all of them contemplated the Bishop. Well, that's the Bishop's phone call to Williams explained, Ian reflected. Poor old man. How appalling it must have been to have to be grateful to Williams.

The Dean cleared his throat. 'I gather you think, Ian, that Mrs Thrigg, our cleaner, may have been one of the participants in these horrid rites?'

Ian mentally shook himself. 'Yes, I think I recognised her going in and I got a shot of her before the candles went out. I rather wonder too if she and Williams might have been involved in transactions with holy water and perhaps candles?'

The Archdeacon flung up his hand and groaned. 'Oh, dear, oh dear, oh dear.'

'Have you any evidence?' asked the Dean grimly. Ian told them about his experience with Julia in the asylum out-building. 'You mean you think the asylum incident had something to do with the black magic people in the Cathedral?'

Ian nodded, 'It's too much of a coincidence to have Cathedral candles up there. There can't be two sets of magicians, surely.'

'I suppose it's something the police will have to look into,' said the Archdeacon wearily.

The Dean nodded agreement and then turned toward Ian.

'And does all this have any connection with the murder of Paul Gray and Canon Wheeler, Ian?'

Ian looked at his boots unhappily.

'Ian,' said the Dean sharply, 'answer my question.'

Ian drew in his breath. The Dean had all the authority which he acknowledged to be present in the Church. He was a priest, an elderly, honourable, intelligent and goodwilled man. He would have liked to tell him all the truth he knew and all that he surmised. But he was inhibited by the fear that his huge hatred of Wheeler would show and make the Dean discount what he said, and perhaps lose him his good opinion.

'About Canon Wheeler,' he compromised at last. 'I'm not sure at the moment how or if he fits into the pattern.'

Ian glanced covertly at Theodora to see if she was going to let him get away with this. He wasn't at all sure how much Theodora surmised about his last meeting with Wheeler on the morning of his death. 'As for a connection with Gray, I think not. I went tonight to watch, as I told you, from Canon Hardnut's house in the expectation that someone would come to collect some candles which had been left there. These candles look like Cathedral candles in that they have the St Manicus arms on them. That they are really Cathedral candles now seems to me to be rather unlikely. If you look at them closely the arms, though accurate, are nowhere near as finely moulded as the ones we've had from Farris's. Moreover if you look closely, the bottom of them is hollow.' Ian produced the St Saviour's candle from his jacket pocket and held it out for the two clerics to see. He went on, 'In the bottom of these candles are hidden quantities of heroin.' He looked at the Dean. 'The person who I think is running the distribution of this drug is Geoffrey Markham.' As he met the Dean's gaze he wondered whether he should add 'your kinsman', and decided not to.

The Dean was silent. In the end the Archdeacon spoke. 'How does Paul Gray fit into this?'

'The possibilities are that he was being used, either wittingly or not, as a distributor through his youth club. If he found out and objected that might be motive enough to,' he paused to select his phrase, 'sever his head from his body.'

The Dean flushed. 'Have you any evidence at all for implicating Markham in this?' Caretaker glanced at the unhappy Dean, then looked at Theodora, who nodded. He told him about the part he suspected Geoffrey had played in the death of the Bishop's son. Then he mentioned the number plate of Gray's car which he and Julia had found at Cumbermound's stables. The Dean and the Archdeacon listened in silence. Finally Ian said formally, 'I would like you to believe that I wish all this were mere fabrication. But I don't feel it is. Moreover, there is the ritual aspect of the severing of a head and the placing of it in a font and returning the sword to the chapel afterwards. None of these actions is that of a sane man. It's flamboyant, actorly stuff, which' — he leaned forward and sought the Dean's eye — 'you know is in Geoffrey's character as it is in his father's.'

The Dean joined his hands together as though in prayer. 'I hope you're wrong. I fear you may not be. Are you going to inform the police or his father or have you indeed already done so?'

'No. I haven't yet. I hoped, as I said, to meet Geoffrey last night. I had some sort of plan of confronting him and' — Ian looked uncomfortable — 'perhaps punishing him if he were doing what I think he is. But now I think I haven't any alternative to letting the police know. His father, I'd rather not do anything about.'

'Do you know where Geoffrey is at the moment?'

'No. I don't. I know he's not at Cumbermound and he's not been seen at his London flat for some weeks. I did check up on both those so, since I've no lead, I think I'd better pass the car number plate over to the police and let them cope.'

'Where is the plate now?'

Theodora bestirred herself. 'Where it is not,' she said, 'is with me. Though it may be that the person who ransacked my room thought I might have it.'

Ian nodded. 'Or he may have been looking for the candles — either the St Saviour's one or the asylum one. They'd be worth a pretty penny. I left the plate, by the way, and the other candle, the one we found in the asylum out-building, with Julia for safekeeping.'

'Where?'

'At her lodgings. Quite safe, I think.'

* * *

Julia gazed with dawning terror at the small, neat figure of Geoffrey Markham. It so closely resembled his father. Markham smiled complacently at Dhani and Julia.

'Don't move,' he said softly. 'My bulging pocket is not mere decoration. Jacob,' he spoke to the Dutchman, 'take friend Jefferson over to the *Merlin* and then come back here with some rope.'

Julia looked at Dhani who was looking at Markham. There were about three yards between them. 'I wouldn't rush it, coon,' Markham said. 'I'd just love to kill you.'

Julia was appalled at the venom of his tone. He couldn't be sane and feel like that, could he?

Twenty minutes later Julia and Dhani found themselves blinking in the surprisingly bright light of the modern saloon of the Dutch yacht next to the *Amy Roy*. It looked more like the bar parlour of a modernised pub than anything nautical. Chrome, plastic and pink glass predominated. The Dutchman stood by the door and Markham surveyed them across the cabin table. Since their hands and feet were both tied they sat awkwardly perched on the bunk edge. Suddenly Markham leant across and with a single finger pushed the unbalanced Dhani sideways from his precarious seat. Dhani crashed helplessly to the floor. Markham yelped with laughter.

'Oh, God,' he said. 'Knocked off your perch, old son.'

He looked closely at Dhani. 'Seen you before, haven't I? At Cambridge. Used to pretend you were an undergraduate. Yes?'

Dhani didn't answer. The Dutchman stepped forward and hauled him back on to the bunk.

'I could be mistaken. All you niggers look alike to me.'

He seemed to lose interest in Dhani and turned to Julia. But before he could speak, Julia demanded, 'Why did you kill my cousin? And why did you hack off his head?'

For a minute Markham looked puzzled. He made no answer. Julia, in spite of her terror, looked closely at him. The pupils were very contracted. The pallor was pronounced and his thinness not disguised by the bulky cotton sailing smock.

'Cousin?'

'Paul Gray.'

'Ah, the priestling. Your cousin, eh? You're prettier than he was. I didn't know you were one of the family. I thought you were just a typist to the fatuous Canon . . . what's his name? Dealer? Wheeler?' Markham rocked backwards and forwards on his feet. 'Both sons of the Lord spiritual methinks. Metaphorically of course. I set one son to look upon the other son. The one was physically blind the other spiritually so. A nice conceit. No? I leave the conundrum with you. And I warned the first son, or I would have done if that bitch of a typist hadn't treated me as though I were a heavy breather. "Canon Wheeler's office" forsooth. Man's a pseud.'

'Why did you kill my cousin?' Julia repeated levelly.

'Kill him? Why should I kill him? I knew no evil of him. Did you?'

Julia didn't answer and after a moment's hesitation Markham turned to the Dutchman. 'Just empty their little pockets, Jacob, there's a good fellow. Try and be slightly more efficient than our good friend Jefferson. He's a little inclined to leave important things behind. The foolish fellow that he is. It'll slow down the process of identification. Never help anyone, let alone the fuzz.'

There was nothing in Dhani's pockets.

'A striking testimony to your simplicity of life,' said Markham.

Julia watched with fascination the changes between sane, rational penetration and the facetious posturing with which it alternated. From Julia's Barbour the Dutchman extracted the asylum candle and the number plate. After a further fumble he came up with Ian's note. These were laid on the table. Markham gazed at them for a moment and flushed with annoyance as their significance became clear to him. Delicately he picked up the candle and then with a sudden movement tapped it on the edge of the cabin table. The bung fell out and a thin trickle of grey powder ran over the polished surface. Dhani's eyes narrowed.

'Busybody Ian, the knight so shining white's been muscling in again I see. I wondered where I'd left my little trophy.' He indicated the plate. Again, Julia wondered whether he was acting or whether, as she suspected, the careless leaving of the number plate was simply another flourish, like putting a head in a font. In the end Geoffrey Markham didn't really care whether he was found out or not. At least half of him wanted to be discovered.

'So you know all,' Markham said in a tone worthy of an early film villain. This time he was certainly acting. 'In that case, it's final good night all round, friends. Tuck them up nice and safe, Jacob, old fruit. No need for night caps though.'

The Dutchman, short and heavy with a square head and square fingers, hesitated between the two of them and finally picked Julia up by her roped hands and feet and carried her aft. She found herself bundled into a locker which appeared to be already full of something which felt like wicker or basket work. There was a pungent, not unpleasant, smell which Julia recognised as incense. A moment later in the intense dark she felt Dhani's light body dumped partly on top of her. Dhani gasped out an apology as he rolled himself off her. Her head appeared to be beside his feet. After a moment the tiny chink of light from the loosely fitting doors of the locker allowed her to see his recumbent form. She was surprised to find that what she mostly felt was anger rather than fear. It was one step on, she thought.

'Dhani, why haven't they killed us yet?'

'I think their resident neck-breaker was out for the count,' said Dhani quaintly employing what he thought was an English idiom. 'And shooting us on the *Amy Roy* might have been noisy. I imagine they'll dump us when they next put to sea.'

'When will that be?' asked Julia who preferred to be killed by a bullet in the head rather than choking to death on sea water.

'If they keep to their regular pattern, on the next tide from Narborough, which is tomorrow, or rather this evening, at about six. I expect we'll be slipping downstream any time during the day.'

'Dhani, what are they up to?'

'As Ian said, it looks like drugs. That stuff he poured on to the table was heroin. The hollows in the candles are stuffed with it.'

'How did they do it?'

'Bring them in from Holland in this boat in consignments of all this Eastern trash.'

Julia had a sudden vision of the stall in the market where she'd seen Mrs Thrigg last Saturday afternoon leaning forward over a pile of just such Eastern trash. 'Dhani,' she said 'the market stall I saw Mrs Thrigg at, the man keeping it had a foreign accent.'

'Dutch?'

'I think so.'

'Well, it would be a good cover. I'll bet there are papers to cover brass, wicker goods and candles perfectly in order. I should imagine, too, most of the candles are OK — drug-free. But some aren't.'

'The ones with the St Manicus arms on them?'

'Right.'

'So, when it comes to sorting them out, the St Manicus arms ones are separated and stowed somewhere and then passed on? To Paul and the youth club?'

'Perhaps.'

'Why?'

'Why not? It's immensely profitable.'

'No. I meant, why the arms of the Cathedral?'

'He's a droll fellow, isn't he? An actor. A jester, wouldn't you say? One for flourishes and gestures. Cocking snooks. He clearly meant Canon Wheeler to find the head in the font.'

'It was Canon Wheeler's month in residence. He'd be due to take Evensong,' Julia chipped in, 'on the Friday afternoon when Mrs Thrigg and I found the head in the font. And the Evensong was scheduled for the St Manicus chapel that day. But why did he want to torment Canon Wheeler with such a sight?'

'"Son sees son",' he said. 'Perhaps he has something against Wheeler or perhaps it's just joking carried that much further — in the same spirit as with the candles. The candle burns for Christ and the bottom holds damnation. That sort of thing.'

'What about the candle on Paul's altar?' asked Julia. If she was going to die she might at least understand how it all happened.

'If Jefferson was a partner in the drugs ring and, though I'm not sure of his motives and I think they may be more complicated than merely money, he clearly was,' said Dhani thoughtfully, 'he might have emptied the drug out of the candles and then simply recycled them in Paul's direction. On the lines of waste not want not. And throwing them away might arouse suspicion.'

'So Paul need not have known about the drugs at all. The candle doesn't necessarily prove that he was implicated.' There was both pleading and relief in Julia's tone. She desperately didn't want her cousin to be guilty.

'It's certainly possible.'

'What about the candles in the asylum out-house? How did a candle find its way there?'

'I wonder if it might not be some sort of black magic. It's easy to see why a black magician might want a candle with the arms of the Cathedral on it. If you're into black arts, you probably want to invert or misuse as many symbols of the orthodox rites as possible. It may be that the group, whoever they are, didn't realise the candles they had contained drugs as well. I was listening carefully to what Markham was saying. Did you notice he said Jefferson wasn't too careful about looking or finding? Some words of that kind.'

Julia nodded and realising Dhani couldn't see her in the blackness, answered, 'Yes.'

'Well, I wondered if that meant that Jefferson had let one or more of the candles slip through, still containing their load of drug. If, say for argument, that had happened on Thursday evening, might not Jefferson and Markham have gone looking for it or them as soon as they realised?'

'Would that be why Jefferson was pursuing me, because I had a candle with drugs in it?'

'It's a probability.'

'I still don't know why they should kill Paul,' Julia said. 'Unless perhaps he found out about the drugs and threatened to go to the police. Nor do I see why they had to kill Canon Wheeler, unless he found out about the drugs too.'

'Actually,' said Dhani, 'if you listened to what Markham said when he mentioned Wheeler, I got the impression that he thought Wheeler was alive. He didn't speak of him in the past tense. You found the body this morning. He may not have seen the evening papers, and if he didn't kill Wheeler there's no reason why he should yet know he's dead. That would mean that someone else killed Wheeler, and if so who and why?'

'It looks,' said Julia tremulously, 'as if we might never know. Dhani, are we going to die?'

'Would you mind?' said Dhani gravely.

'I'm not sure. No. Yes. I think I mind how I die and I hate to see bullies get away with it. Joking, manipulating, coercing and killing — I don't want to be a victim of that. I'm sick of being a victim.' She paused. 'I don't suppose Paul wanted to die. He shouldn't have been put in a position where he had no choice. No one should.' She fell silent at the prospect.

'Holding, as I do, a doctrine of ahimsa,' said Dhani theoretically, 'I'm surprised to find how very much I agree with you. Perhaps it's my English schooling. Independent schools are hierarchies and hierarchies licence a certain amount of bullying so that the products tend to feel it's all right. I myself look for a commonwealth of free, rational and equal beings and for that reason,' he grunted and Julia felt his body first become tense and then relax beside hers, 'I intend to slip my collar and see what can be done.'

With amazement, Julia felt his hand on her feet. 'How?'

'Oriental cunning,' said Dhani complacently. 'I imagine the combat expert who is *hors de combat* would not have made the mistakes which the square Dutchman did with knots.'

When they were both free and had recovered from the surprising pain of restored circulation, Dhani said, 'It's still dark. The last bell I heard from the Cathedral clock struck two. We don't know if they've left anyone on guard. I think it would be safest to swim for it. You do swim, don't you?'

'Yes,' said Julia firmly, quelling her fear of drowning. She knew she was competent, if not keen.

'If either of us makes it,' said Dhani carefully, 'the first phone box or the first policemen. No more beggaring about with self-help. Time the professionals did their bit. I've had enough of rough houses. I always thought England was such an orderly country.'

Julia found herself giggling. 'I thought so too. I've seen some terrible pub fights in Australia and I haven't seen one in England.'

'It has other ways of being violent.'

Julia thought of Wheeler's bullying and then of his broken neck. The Cathedral clock struck the half.

'Right,' said Dhani quietly, 'Let's push off.'

CHAPTER TEN: EARTH UPON EARTH HAS SET ALL HIS THOUGHT

'Ian Henry Caretaker, I arrest you for the murder of Charles Victor Wheeler. I have to warn you that you do not need to say anything but that anything you do say may be taken down and used in evidence.'

Tallboy's tone was gruff with triumph. His clothes appeared to fit him even less well than usual. The two constables closed in on either side of Caretaker. It was Tuesday morning. The culmination of two hours further questioning by the police in the conference room of St Manicus house had been Tallboy absenting himself for fifteen minutes and returning to make his charge.

Ian smiled at him kindly, with genuine fellow feeling. 'Yes,' he said. 'I thought you might. However, before you do anything rash' — he leaned forwards towards Tallboy — 'anything which might be detrimental to your career, might I suggest that you call a meeting of the Dean, Archdeacon, Bishop, even Deaconess Braithwaite and perhaps Miss Smith? If you like you could bring your heavies with you to make sure I don't make a break for it.'

Ian indicated the two seemingly twelve-year-old constables standing beside him. He tried to keep the contempt out of his voice because, after all, it wasn't their fault that they had a dolt for their boss.

'I can assure you,' said Tallboy heavily, 'I am acting on the full authority of the Superintendent and the Chief Constable. And the Bishop knows,' he added defensively. 'Moreover, may I remind you that' — exasperation got the better of him — 'everything you say is being taken down.' He looked at the WPC who was scribbling away with every appearance of interest.

'Yes, yes, yes,' said Caretaker. 'I hope she got that bit about your career.'

'Constable, take this man back to the station,' said Tallboy.

Ian said calmly, 'In the top drawer of my desk, you will find a candle with the St Manicus arms on its base.'

'Yes,' Tallboy interrupted him with satisfaction. 'We've got it. You'll be charged with offences under the Possession of Drugs Act as well as murder in due course.'

Ian felt all the anger which for years he'd suppressed or diverted swell up in him. The fatigue he had felt after his nocturnal exertions left him. He reverted to the diction of his prep school. 'How can you be so dense, you dunderhead? Haven't you got anyone with any nous in your flat-footed crew?'

Tallboy had no intention of finding out what 'nous' meant. He jerked his head at the two constables. 'What are you waiting for?'

The constables closed their grip on Ian's arms and began to propel him towards the door. Taller than either of them, he allowed himself to be moved forward for three paces and then stopped dead and swung round. 'And if you let anything happen to Miss Smith,' he said, 'I'll not merely break your career, I'll break your neck too.'

* * *

Theodora propped her tall self uneasily against the dark wood panelling of the entrance hall of the Bishop's Palace. She felt extremely nervous. There was no rational justification for her fear, she thought. Her conscience was clear. She was not stupid or ill-willed. She was simply doing what had to be done. Why, then, this irrational sinking of the heart? The Bishop's authority derived from his office not his person. But at this point she was stuck, for the Bishop, as she well knew, was frightening in virtue of his person not his office. She began to pray one of the two psalms for that morning: 'Go not far from me, O God. My God haste thee to help me.'

Theodora had learned of Ian's prolonged questioning by the police from Mary, the receptionist. She had seen the Inspector and his crew summon Ian to the conference room as soon as he had come in. They had also searched Ian and Theodora's room thoroughly. Julia had not come in and there had been no phone call asking for leave of absence. When she had gathered all this, Theodora had telephoned downstairs.

'Canon Wheeler's office,' answered Miss Coldharbour's voice, no less poised than when her superior had been alive.

'Miss Coldharbour, I'd like to see you at once please,' Theodora had said. 'Would you come up to my office?'

There had been the slightest of pauses and then Miss Coldharbour's tone, which perhaps had a touch of constraint in it, had responded, 'Of course, Miss Braithwaite. I'll be with you in a moment.'

Miss Coldharbour, when she had appeared a few minutes later, had looked, Theodora thought, tired and older than ever before. Theodora had fixed her with her own honest eye and said, 'Now, Miss Coldharbour, about money.'

I wonder what on earth possessed the two of them, thought Theodora, as she gazed at the Bishop's arms carved into the lintel over his study door. Suddenly the door was opened by the Bishop's diminutive secretary who murmured, 'The Bishop will see you now.'

Theodora took a grip on herself and strode into the rather small room. A lot of modern fumed-oak panelling gave it the air of a 1930s liner and there were several horrible reproduction club chairs haphazardly arranged. One almost expected to see chromium ashtrays in leather straps over their arms.

The Bishop was turned away from her, seated in his chair in the bay window, staring out towards the Cathedral. There was an air of lethargy about him and Theodora caught a glimpse of his feet propped on a footstool. He was wearing, as was his right, a purple cassock. Purple for royalty and purple for the colour of dried blood, Theodora thought. She took up her stand mid-stage and waited. It was some moments before he turned stiffly towards her. His large, square, heavy face with its small eyes betrayed no emotion. He fixed his attention on her.

'Well?'

'Ian Caretaker.'

'Killed, I am told, Charles Wheeler.'

'I think not.'

'The police tell me his fingerprints are all over the office.' The Bishop paused. 'He had, apparently, the opportunity and the motive in that he had some sort of quarrel, no one seems to be too sure about what, immediately prior to Charles being found dead. Why should you suppose the police wrong?'

'I don't say that Ian couldn't have killed Canon Wheeler. What I do feel sure about, after working with him for four years, is that if he had killed him, he would have confessed at once. He'd have gone to the nearest policeman or, more likely, rung the Dean.'

'I commend your loyalty to your colleague. I would remind you, however, that your first loyalty is to the Church in this diocese.'

And all its crooked members, thought Theodora. 'Charles didn't care for Ian and Ian did not care for Charles,' she said. 'That's not a motive for murder.'

'I need not remind you that I appointed Canon Wheeler to his canonry here.'

It would need the mind of a priest, Theodora thought, to make a connection between that remark and what they were talking about: Wheeler was a priest, so the Bishop would support him; Caretaker wasn't so he wouldn't. She made one last try.

'Bishop, Ian is in difficulties and needs our,' she took a breath, 'your, support.'

The Bishop regarded her steadily giving no trace of having heard her. Theodora pressed on.

'I wonder if you knew that Canon Wheeler was in financial difficulties?'

The Bishop gave a slight sigh of impatience. 'I hardly think it proper for you to speculate on Canon Wheeler's private affairs.'

Theodora stiffened at this cruelty. 'The quarrel between Canon Wheeler and Ian was that Ian had discovered that there were funds missing from the appeals account. Ian felt that Canon Wheeler could help him to clear the matter up.'

'I fail to understand you.'

'Canon Wheeler had been transferring appeals funds to his own account.'

'I find such a suggestion preposterous.'

'What Canon Wheeler was doing, apparently,' Theodora continued feigning calmness, 'was transferring amounts from one account to another. Only bits got left off in the course of the transference. It was only possible, Ian says, because we haven't had a full-time appeals secretary since Canon Wheeler dismissed the last man. And of course, the Comptroller, as you know, recently died and the diocesan secretary has a sabbatical.' She paused and then resumed. 'It is possible, too, that Charles felt that what he was doing was obtaining a loan from the Church rather than actually stealing.' That, thought, Theodora, had been Miss Coldharbour's line when she had questioned her.

'Supposing that Caretaker is right, which I do not suppose to be the case, why should Charles do such a thing?'

'He had,' said Theodora carefully, 'rather a lot of calls on his resources.'

'Hardly more than the rest of us,' said the Bishop bitterly. Theodora had noticed this general attitude of senior clergy of drawing away their skirts when the vulgarity of money raised its head. Theodora restrained herself from pointing out to the Bishop that Canon Wheeler had lived like a nineteenth-century cleric. He had kept a considerable establishment, entertained in London as well as in Medewich. In his dress, his table, his cellar and his diversions, he had striven to recommend himself in every possible way as a candidate for a bishopric. Instead she said, 'He had two households to support.'

'I hardly think a cottage on the Cumbermound estate would be an excessive drain on his resources.'

'Canon Wheeler supported a wife in Glasgow.'

For a second what might have been pain registered on the Bishop's face. The saurian eyes glittered as they raked Theodora up and down. 'I understood Canon Wheeler to be unmarried.'

'He married when he was twenty-two, a year before he came south and some six years before he entered the priesthood.'

'You have proof?'

'Yes,' said Theodora bleakly.

'Yes, I suppose so. But why not admit the marriage? We are not a celibate priesthood. I suppose he *was* married?'

'Yes. He was married in a Glasgow registry office, his wife being a Roman Catholic.'

'That's no bar. Rather the contrary nowadays,' said the Bishop regretfully.

'I understand,' said Theodora, hating herself for saying this, 'that Mrs Wheeler is not a woman who seeks the limelight. She has simple tastes.' Mrs Gaskell would have done better Theodora thought. She also thought how much more comfortable she'd feel if she could sit down.

'You mean Wheeler didn't think her presentable,' snapped the Bishop suddenly. 'That's absolute nonsense,' he added, 'these days.'

Theodora thought about it and decided that it had to be done. The Bishop wasn't more self-deluding than many men but he certainly wasn't less so. Moreover, his snobbery was renowned beyond the boundaries of the diocese. He had, too, been in office for a long time. It narrowed, thought Theodora sadly, their sympathies as well as their perspective. 'Not such great nonsense for anyone ambitious for the highest offices in the Church, as I think Canon Wheeler might have been,' she finally said.

She watched a flush spread over the parchment face as the significance of her remark went home, surprised to find how little pity she had for the Bishop as she went in deeper. She thought of all the people whose lives Wheeler had made miserable by his rough arrogance, his pleasure in humiliating, his enjoyment of silly small persecutions. He was your placeman she thought. You picked him and put him there and supported him. Your values infected him. Wheeler was terrified of departing from them or failing to meet them. The responsibility for Charles Wheeler is partly yours. He kept bad company.

It was almost as if the Bishop had read her thoughts. 'He could always have come to me,' he said, as though defending himself. 'He should have come to me. I'd have helped.'

Charles was totally insecure morally, socially, intellectually and spiritually, were the words that sprang into Theodora's head but she modified them into, 'I think Canon Wheeler lacked confidence in himself and so did not, perhaps, at all points entirely trust his colleagues' opinion of him.'

'Faith,' announced the Bishop, whether in summary of Wheeler's lack or as a first-person exhortation, Theodora did not know.

'What connection does all this have with his death?' The Bishop's voice had that slightly nasal bray which afflicted him when he had preached on too many occasions in a single day.

'I hope you will believe,' said Theodora formally, 'that I offer you this information not simply to accuse Canon Wheeler. The point is that in two areas of his life Canon Wheeler was doing something out of role, things certain to generate their own tensions. They would bring him enemies and contacts which were far more likely to provide motives for violence, even murder, than any mere office feuding.' As she said this Theodora was aware of a certain disingenuousness in her utterance. The bullying of hapless subordinates was one of a piece with depriving his wife of her proper place in society and with taking other people's money to further his own ambitious showiness. But she let it rest.

The Bishop was clearly beginning to tire. His hands, like an old woman's, were tapping restlessly on the arms of his chair. At that point the telephone rang. There was a minute's pause while, presumably, the secretary in the office next door fielded the call. Theodora moved her weight from her right foot to her left, reclasped her sweating hands behind her and fixed her eye on the Cathedral tower outside the Bishop's window. Finally, the buzzer rasped on the internal telephone on the Bishop's desk. The Bishop fixed it with his eye, lifted his gaze to Theodora and dropped it back to the telephone.

Theodora stepped forward to the desk and lifted the receiver. 'Bishop's office. Theodora Braithwaite here.'

After a moment she raised her eyes to the Bishop and said, 'It's Superintendent Frost of Medewich CID. He is with Mr Caretaker in Canon Wheeler's office. He wonders whether he could have a word with you. Should he come to you or would you find it possible to step across to St Manicus house?'

The Bishop glared at Theodora with perfect unfriendliness. At last, with some difficulty, he rose from his chair and reached for his stick. Theodora murmured into the telephone, 'The Bishop will be with you shortly, Superintendent.'

With a smile that had much warmth in it she opened the door for him.

* * *

Inspector Tallboy's heavies were just considering the problem of collapsing Ian Caretaker into the squad car outside the diocesan office when the Superintendent's seven-year-old Ford swerved to a halt in front of it. There was a pause before the Superintendent got out. Tallboy, who had appeared on the steps of the office, hurried forward to greet his superior, in his eagerness pushing his face into the open window of the Ford.

'Good morning, sir. We've just made the arrest.'

'I feared you would have,' said Frost dourly.

Tallboy's heart sank, remembering Caretaker's remarks about his career. Suddenly he felt the real unfairness of the world crowd in on him. 'But you said . . .' His voice was like a schoolboy's, high with indignant self-justification.

'Yes, yes, yes,' said Frost testily. 'New information. We had a call from the girl, Miss Smith, and her chap, Mr Tambiah. What they had to tell us casts a rather different light on things. We've also got Jefferson but not yet Markham. I really can't think why people, especially Mr Caretaker, didn't come clean long ago.' He fixed his codfish eye on Tallboy. 'You couldn't help it, I'm sure,' he said unkindly.

Frost got out of the Ford and signalled to the two waiting PCs who released Ian's arms and abandoned the struggle to fit him neatly into a space for which he was patently too tall. The Superintendent strolled in leisurely fashion across to the squad car and, leaning his elbow companionably on it, gazed up into Ian's face several inches above his own.

'Good morning, Mr Caretaker,' he said genially. 'And a very pleasant one it is too.' He gestured in the direction of the scudding and overcast sky. Caretaker glowered at him.

'Really?'

'Yes, indeed. I wondered,' he began elaborately, 'if you could possibly spare us a moment of your valuable time.' Ian was not disposed to help him out.

'I thought I was under arrest.'

The Superintendent stroked his chin and ran his forefinger across the neat bristle of his moustache, a parody of the gesture of thinking. 'Well, I suppose, technically. However, one or two things have cropped up fairly recently. Failure in communication.' He gestured vaguely in the direction of Tallboy as though he were a species of out-of-order field telephone.

'It would,' he said winningly, 'help us an awful lot if you could forget the arrest bit and join us in a little informal discussion.'

'I'd like a solicitor,' said Ian unforgivingly.

'Round a table, as it were,' wheedled the Superintendent. 'We wouldn't want a shorthand writer. In fact there wouldn't be anyone else but me.'

Ian hesitated.

'You, I imagine, might well like the Dean and the Archdeacon here and perhaps,' he added, as though offering a special treat to a recalcitrant child at a tea table, 'in time, the Bishop and Miss Braithwaite?'

'Where?' said Ian.

'I think,' said Frost, disguising his relief, 'Canon Wheeler's office would be appropriate.'

* * *

Frost marched, apparently without a tremor, to Wheeler's chair and moved it slightly to one side. As he did so he glanced at the Masaccio copy and sucked his teeth appreciatively. 'Lovely brushwork, very skilful copy, wouldn't you say, Dean?'

The Dean nodded curtly. He looked tired after his night's exertions. He was sure no good would be coming to the Church in the near future.

Ian took his usual bentwood chair in front of Canon Wheeler's desk and leaned back. His head ached from last night's fighting. He felt stiff all over and his longing for coffee was extreme. But, he told himself, there was now light at the end of the tunnel. 'I think,' he said, 'it would save time if the Bishop and Miss Braithwaite were here.'

'Ah, yes, of course.' Frost was all compliance. He picked up the telephone.

They all gazed at the ceiling or out of the window or at the appalling picture of Marsyas. It felt like the end of the world, thought Ian. At last the sound of the Bishop's stick could be heard on the stairs and the door opened. Everyone rose. The Bishop greeted no one and Frost was obviously not going to offer him his chair. Theodora and the Archdeacon came in together, wheeling another armchair forward and placing it opposite Frost.

'Well now,' said Frost, when they were all seated. 'I understand Miss Smith and Mr Tambiah are safe, and the information they have is with me. It has some light to throw on certain parties concerned with the events of the last fortnight. However, I think, Mr Caretaker, it falls to you to start us off, since you are especially concerned with the death of Canon Wheeler.'

'I'm not sure how much you know,' said Ian to Frost. 'Would you like to start by asking questions and I'll do my best to answer them as fully as possible?' His tone to Frost had softened. The man was no longer a bully exercising power, a superior claiming rank.

'I wonder if we could get Canon Wheeler out of the way first. Could you put us straight about the events of the morning of his murder? Monday morning. Yesterday morning, in fact, though I'm sure it seems a long time ago to you. You came into the office earlier than usual?'

'Yes, I was in by eight.'

'Why?'

'I had a difficult interview with Canon Wheeler ahead and I wanted to have all the facts prepared before confronting him.'

'These facts concerned his use of certain Cathedral funds?'

'Yes.'

'When you came in at eight, you went straight to your office?'

Ian hesitated. But there was no longer any point in trying to conceal the fact which had probably led to his arrest. Best let everything come out and trust to Theodora to provide the missing bits. 'No,' he said reluctantly. 'I entered by the back door which leads straight from the car park and came up the backstairs to the first-floor landing. Then I went into Canon Wheeler's room.'

'Why?'

'I knew that somewhere Wheeler kept a file of his monetary transactions which would provide me with proof of his having had his hand in the till. And a motive for his actions.'

'So you thought it permissible to enter and search your superior's room while he was out and ferret amongst his private papers?' said the Dean with immense distaste.

Ian blushed. All that he had feared, all that had kept him from broaching matters earlier, had come to pass and the result had been just as he expected: he had lost the Dean's respect. The fact that Wheeler himself had not scrupled to search his colleagues' rooms or that he might be guilty of fraud, did not for a moment excuse Ian's conduct in the Dean's gentlemanly eyes.

'How did you know such information might be found in his room?' the Superintendent asked in a neutral tone.

Theodora entered the conversation like a well-practised relay runner, suavely taking up the baton from the unhappy Ian. 'The information came, I think I am right in saying' — she glanced at Ian for confirmation — 'from Miss Coldharbour, whom, I gather, you saw on Sunday night after the Medewich and Markham Agricultural Show.'

Ian nodded. 'Yes. I went to see her after Julia and I had found the number plate of Paul Gray's car in the stables at Cumbermound.'

'Why should you suppose that Miss Coldharbour would know about Gray's number plate?' asked Frost judiciously.

'I didn't. I thought that Geoffrey Markham knew about the number plate and I further supposed that Markham's connection with Gray would mean drugs.' He glanced at the Bishop. 'I'd found such a connection to hold in the past.'

Frost nodded. 'Your connection was correct. What we have learned from Mr Tambiah and Miss Smith suggests that Markham was bringing in large quantities of drugs from Holland in his boat, the *Merlin*. They were hidden in the bases of candles specially marked with the diocesan arms. These were being distributed by Jefferson.'

The Archdeacon frowned. 'I would never have supposed it of Jefferson. We had a word with him, of course, after the affair at Narborough and I formed the impression that he was a remarkably upright man. Someone with a real, if rather narrow, moral concern.'

Frost nodded in agreement. 'We've had an opportunity to question Jefferson and he is indeed a very odd sort of man. He's not interested in money. One of the things he does in the course of his youth training sessions is to institute his own private merit badge for character development. It's part of a healthy mind in healthy body approach. He teaches combat techniques for the body and exposes them to the temptation of taking drugs to develop moral stamina. If they fall to the temptation they've failed. They aren't competent to deal with life, in Jefferson's opinion. It's so bizarre that no one quite believed it when he tried it the first time round in Narborough. Hence the difficulty of pinning witnesses down and making out a case against him. Normal vice we can deal with; abnormal virtue is rather beyond us.' Frost folded his arms and looked towards Ian again. The Bishop too turned his stony gaze on Ian.

Ian pressed on. 'We knew, I mean Theodora and Julia and Dhani and I knew, that Canon Wheeler had a list of people on whom he was keeping a sort of file. Julia found it,' Ian said defensively to the Dean, 'by accident when she was waiting at the dinner party at Canon Wheeler's last Friday night. The names on the list were Gray, Markham, Williams, Jefferson and my own. I've puzzled over the connections which might exist between them. The problem is, we don't know *when* the list was made, the only thing I think we have in common is that we might all in our different ways have been able to afford Wheeler some of his particular sort of sport.'

'Sport,' said the Dean sharply.

'He was a bully. He liked inspiring fear. If I'm honest, *I* feared him. It's irrational, as these things are, but I did. I think it's possible the list was nothing more than Wheeler's game book.'

The Bishop looked with distaste at Ian who, however, continued. 'When I heard Markham's name was on the list, I began to recall his past history. I wondered what the relationship was between Wheeler and Markham. I wondered whether Wheeler was implicated in the drugs ring. After all, he had a cottage on the Cumbermound estate. I thought the person who knew most about Canon Wheeler and his finances was Rosamund Coldharbour. If Wheeler was supplementing his income either by running drugs or blackmailing someone else for running them, she'd know. So I went to see her. I think Theodora knows what I found.'

'I had a word,' said Theodora briskly, 'this morning with Miss Coldharbour. In his search of Canon Wheeler's room Ian did not find the papers for which he was looking. Miss Coldharbour had kept these with her own files. All Ian succeeded in doing was leaving his fingerprints all over Canon Wheeler's desk.' Theodora felt a slight edge in her voice at Ian's inefficiency. Though of course, she conceded to herself, he could not have known that Canon Wheeler was going to be killed and his room consequently searched.

'It seems to me,' she went on, 'that Miss Coldharbour has been under a considerable strain for some time now. She is, as Ian has told us, conversant with Canon Wheeler's affairs and has up to now been intensely loyal to him. It had, however, become increasingly apparent to her of late, that these affairs were tangled and not as innocent as they ought to be. The strain of divided loyalties began to tell. In a way Ian visited her at the crucial moment on Sunday night. And the additional shock of Wheeler's death prompted her to give me a little more information. What she revealed to me was three facts. Firstly, she showed me the evidence for Canon Wheeler's having transferred money from the Cathedral Appeal account to his own account.'

The Dean frowned.

'Secondly, she showed me the evidence for his having a wife and a second establishment to support in Glasgow.'

The Bishop sighed.

'And thirdly she told me that when she first discovered the monetary fraud, she called in Paul Gray.'

The Archdeacon's face registered comprehension. 'Paul trained as an accountant before he entered the priesthood.'

'Just so.' Theodora smiled at him. 'Wheeler had, of course, been extraordinarily careless, or else arrogant, in his way of getting money. It seems to have escaped his notice that Rosamund handled all his affairs and that she had all the information to make the inference which Ian too made when he studied the figures carefully. But Charles's attitude was that Rosamund was a typist so she couldn't possibly have the knowledge of an accountant. However, she did have information and she was worried enough to go to Gray whom she had known as a curate at Narborough for some confirmation.'

'Why didn't she go through the proper channels?' said the Dean testily.

'I think she may not have known what the proper channels were for accusing a Canon of stealing.'

'She could have come to any of the Chapter, the Archdeacon or myself or the Bishop.'

Caretaker and Theodora were constrained to exchange glances. Theodora said, 'She may have been frightened to do any of those things. She might have been afraid of being wrong, of looking foolish or worse, or losing her post or finding it intolerable to continue in it, if she were. She may too,' Theodora added carefully, 'have known how very difficult it is for laymen to present new facts to the clergy, particularly when one of their number is involved.'

'What connection,' said the Archdeacon, tactfully trying to change the subject, 'has this with Canon Wheeler's death?'

Frost looked at Ian. 'What did you do after you'd searched Canon Wheeler's desk this morning at eight o'clock?'

'I went for a walk.'

'Why?'

'Social awkwardness. I had an appointment to see Wheeler at half-past ten. I didn't relish meeting him before that time.'

'When did you fix that appointment?'

'I rang him at his home on Sunday night.'

'Did you tell Canon Wheeler why you wanted to see him?'

'I said a financial matter of some importance.'

'What did he say?'

'"I cannot spare you more than five minutes. I'm up to my eyes at the moment."' Caretaker's voice was a tastelessly good imitation of Wheeler's at his most pompous.

'So you went out for a walk and returned when?'

'Yes. I walked round the Cathedral and returned through the back door from the car park about twenty past ten.'

'What happened at the interview?'

'Wheeler denied everything. Challenged me to produce evidence, of which of course, I could only produce part, namely the figures which he denied had the significance which I had given them. He ended by telling me I could expect my cards at the end of the month. In fact it was a very typical exercise in Wheeler's favourite technique of frightening people off.'

'And what was your reaction?'

'I intended to get hold of Miss Coldharbour and go to the Dean with the evidence. Before I did that, as I told your inspector, I went down to the Secretary's office to see if I could find anything more on the appeals account. There was no one in that office so you have only my word for it that I was there from about half-past eleven, after my interview with Wheeler, until Theodora rang me at about half-past twelve with news of Wheeler's murder.'

'May I ask you,' Frost said, 'when you went out this morning for your walk before your interview with Canon Wheeler, did you go out through the back door into the car park?'

'Yes.'

'And did you happen to notice who was parked there?'

'Well, there is only parking space for four cars. The Dean and the Archdeacon both keep their cars there and my own has a space, plus one other which is shared between Mary and Rosamund Coldharbour. Rosamund wasn't in so Mary had it.'

'Did you see any other car parked there?'

'There wouldn't have been . . .' Caretaker trailed off. 'There was a motorbike there,' he said. 'Largish, oldish.'

Frost nodded with pleasure. 'Yes,' he said. 'Inspector Tallboy should be charging Jefferson now. A task, I think, within his capacity.' He smiled at Ian in a friendly fashion.

Ian looked puzzled. 'Why should Jefferson kill Wheeler?'

'Before we go into that,' said Frost, 'may I ask you why you went to Canon Hardnut's last night?'

'In the light of Mrs Baggley's remarks about having seen Markham in Canons' Court on Thursday night, I wanted to track him down and see if he could provide me with information about a connection between himself and Wheeler and Gray in the matter of drugs. Once I'd verified the fact that both the asylum candle and the one from St Saviour's had false bottoms and were carrying drugs I naturally thought of Markham. I surmised that he might have used Canon Hardnut's as a place to keep candles in before passing them via Jefferson to Gray. I later realised that it wasn't as simple as that. However, I think Theodora can fill us in on the real connection.'

'Miss Braithwaite?'

'You must understand that I am relying partly on the testimony of Mrs Baggley and partly on that of Mrs Thrigg, with whom I've had a word, combined with one or two inferences which I have made from what Mrs Gray said. I rather think, Superintendent, that you've already gathered similar information?'

'I should be most happy if you could guide us through the maze, Miss Braithwaite,' said Frost gallantly.

'The clue,' said Theodora thoughtfully, 'is in the comings and goings at Canons' Court on the Thursday night before Gray's death. We're almost certain that he was bidden by Canon Wheeler to make one of his periodical appearances.' She turned to the Dean. 'Canon Wheeler was in the habit of requiring Gray to see him to receive advice about his running of his parish and in particular his youth club.'

'What on earth for?' said the Archdeacon in bewilderment. 'Wheeler had no experience himself in running either. His ministry had been almost entirely in cathedrals.'

'I don't think that would have occurred to Charles. Whereas the pleasures of giving advice and admonition to a younger man were, we know, attractive to him.' The Bishop looked as though he were about to say something and then changed his mind.

Frost interrupted the fractious clergy. 'Do please go on, Miss Braithwaite.'

'We know he left home about six in the evening, without having cancelled his youth club and having made a phone call. I think the phone call was to Jefferson and it was to tell him to pick him up from Wheeler's after his interview with him. He did not cancel the youth club because he didn't expect to have to miss it. His expectation was that he would see Wheeler and then go back with Jefferson in the usual way to Markham cum Cumbermound. But he didn't get to Wheeler's on time. Did his car break down, Superintendent?'

Frost nodded. 'Oil on his clothes and on his hands suggests it.'

'The only people whose movements we can testify to in Canons' Court that night are Mrs Thrigg, who came and went to a variety of houses and was seen and to some extent timed by Mrs Baggley, and Geoffrey Markham who was also seen by Mrs Baggley and, by inference from his motorbike, Jefferson.'

'Quite right, Miss Braithwaite.' said Frost.

'First Mrs Thrigg. She arrived about seven and went to Wheeler's to leave some shopping for the morrow. In the course of that visit she heard Wheeler and Gray quarrelling. While they were still quarrelling, Mrs Thrigg left and went to help Mrs Baggley with her Church Army coffee. What Mrs Thrigg didn't reveal to Mrs Baggley but what I'm certain now she did do, was to return after the end of the party and leave some candles in Canon Hardnut's house. Large altar candles which she had picked up from the market stall and was accustomed to leave in Hardnut's to which she had the key for cleaning and caretaking purposes.'

'Why on earth should she do that?' asked the Archdeacon.

'She was, as you now know, one of the black magicians who intended to use the Cathedral for a ritual on Monday, the ritual which Ian disturbed. Canon Hardnut's was handy for the Cathedral. The candles were awkward to carry around, being about three foot long and fairly thick. It might provoke comment if they were seen in the environs of the Cathedral.'

The Archdeacon broke in, 'But if she wanted candles for her nasty rites why didn't she use the Cathedral ones which Williams could get for her?'

'I think they may have done so at first,' said Ian, 'but when I questioned Williams he told me that Canon Wheeler had been checking up on quantities. They may have thought it too dangerous to continue using the proper ones and so looked for alternative sources of supply.'

Ian returned the conversation to Theodora who continued, 'What Mrs Baggley did not know was that these particular candles had, as a result of Jefferson's mistake, not been relieved of the drugs they contained in their base. You know that, don't you, Inspector, because I'm sure you've found that the ones your men picked up from the floor of the Cathedral after the magic rites had heroin in their bases?'

Frost smiled warmly. 'Quite right, Miss Braithwaite. Our information from Mr Tambiah is that the Dutch cruiser, *Merlin*, brings in consignments of eastern goods every ten days from Holland. Amongst the brass and wicker goods are the fake St Manicus candles with heroin in their bases. They are emptied and then sold on from the market stall or recycled by Jefferson on to churches connected with his youth work. Only on this occasion, Jefferson was careless and a packet of unemptied candles was sold. Is that not so, Miss Braithwaite?'

Theodora took up the narrative again. 'I surmise that as soon as Jefferson realised that a packet of full candles had been sold from the market stall to the general public, in this case Mrs Thrigg, he phoned Markham and set off in pursuit of them some time after the stall had closed on Thursday evening. The stall owner knew Mrs Thrigg since he'd sold her various things before. Jefferson caught up with her but of course had no opportunity to get back the candles. So, he trailed her and hung about Canons' Court waiting for her. Mrs Baggley, you remember, saw his machine illicitly parked. The last thing which Mrs Thrigg did when she had finished at Mrs Baggley's was to go to Canon Hardnut's and dump the candles ready to be picked up on Monday evening, the night of the full moon.'

Ian broke in, 'So I was wrong to think Markham and Jefferson habitually used Hardnut's as a cache for storing heroin candles.'

'Yes. You picked the right house for the wrong reason. The cache was Mrs Thrigg's not Markham's. He had no need for a second staging post. The market stall was enough.' Theodora pressed on. 'Markham and Jefferson entered Hardnut's after her departure and were in the process of looking for them when they were interrupted.'

Theodora paused. 'We have to remember that we left Paul Gray having one of his monthly sessions with Canon Wheeler.' And I can just imagine how it would go and the tone Charles would use, Theodora thought, lecturing, instructing, hectoring the younger man as though he were a pupil, Gray unsure how far Wheeler's authority extended, or whether it was backed by the Bishop himself, unsure too of the purity of his own motives. She continued steadily. 'Mrs Thrigg, you remember, told Mrs Baggley that Mr Gray and Canon Wheeler were having a set-to about a woman and money. Topics on which Mrs Thrigg thought it quite proper for gentlemen to be quarrelling. I think that what this means is that when Charles started in on Paul, Paul finally lost his temper and used the two bits of evidence against Wheeler which Miss Coldharbour had supplied to him, namely his marriage and his stealing funds.'

'Then what?'

'If you search Canon Wheeler's house, Superintendent,' Ian broke in, 'and then look at Canon Hardnut's, I think you'll see what happened next. When Julia was using it last Friday night she noticed that the balustrade of Canon Wheeler's back staircase had been broken away and pushed back into place without too much conviction. And on the floor of Canon Hardnut's hall you'll find, I think, traces of blood from Gray's body.'

'If you're lucky,' Theodora concluded, 'you might even find Canon Wheeler's fingerprints in Canon Hardnut's hall. I don't suppose Charles thought ahead enough to wear gloves.'

The Bishop leaned forward in the grip of strong emotion. 'I refuse to believe that a Canon of the Church of England in this diocese could cut off a fellow priest's head and put it in a font.'

Ian restrained himself from saying he had no such difficulties of belief. He had been following Theodora's narration with close attention and he felt he was now in a position to make one or two inferences on his own account. 'I don't think he did,' he said, 'I think Wheeler saw his future bishopric disappearing over the horizon when he heard Gray's accusation. To produce a nondescript wife twenty-five years after you've married her, would look eccentric even by the standards of the Church of England. For it to be known that you had had your hand in the till to keep yourself in claret might, too, be rather difficult to hush up, even given the Church's resources. I think Wheeler panicked.'

Frost intervened. 'I mentioned that we've questioned Jefferson,' he said. 'Canon Wheeler may certainly not have meant to kill Gray. But he did force him out on to his back staircase. Whether he meant to break his neck we shall never know. And he certainly did convey the body to Canon Hardnut's because Jefferson, and I expect Markham when we lay our hands on him, will bear this out, saw him bring the body into Hardnut's. They were both there, as you surmised, Miss Braithwaite, looking for their drug candles at about midnight. They'd found one. But Mrs Thrigg had bought more than that and had put them in different places. Naturally they were eager to recover as many as possible. The delay was long enough for them to observe Wheeler dumping the body.'

'Then,' said Ian to Frost, 'I suppose it was Markham who conceived the idea of frightening Wheeler and informing him that his action had been witnessed by severing Gray's head and putting it in the font? Markham would know about the Bishop's door and might guess about how often' — Ian chose his words carefully, not daring to glance at the Bishop — 'it was locked. I'm sure it was he who returned the sword and he certainly used the Bishop's door for that. Wheeler was in residence this month and so due to take Evensong as one of his duties. To make sure, Markham rang his office but failed to get through to him, owing to the protective activities of Miss Coldharbour.'

'Why,' asked the Dean grimly, 'would he go to such elaborate trouble?'

'Partly out of mischief, tormenting Wheeler, and partly out of its being useful to have someone in a position of power whom he could blackmail. Also it might deflect interest away from drug-filled candles and make us think about motives stemming from ritual murder.'

'Why put his body in the compost heap?'

'To make sure that it was, in the end, found. Again they couldn't point you in the direction of Canon Hardnut's without there being a danger that the other drugged candle would be discovered.'

'While we're on the subject of phone calls,' said Frost, 'do I gather the Archdeacon has been receiving malicious ones?'

The Archdeacon roused himself from abstraction. 'I think they may be part of the activities of the unhappy Mrs Thrigg and her fellow magicians. In retrospect I recognised her voice.'

'Ah, yes,' said Frost meditatively. 'That would figure.'

'What about Paul's car?' asked Ian.

'I should think we'll find it,' Frost obliged him, 'at one of those breakers on the Medewich to Markham cum Cumbermound road on the other side of the river. Markham could have taken it the same night.'

'What about Wheeler's death?' asked the Archdeacon. 'You say Jefferson did it. Why?'

Frost took the explanation upon himself. 'Jefferson has this odd sense of morality. He genuinely liked Gray, though he thought him weak. He also thinks that there is such a thing as justice as a sort of equilibrium. An eye for an eye. Wheeler had killed. It was his plain duty to kill Wheeler in return. Jefferson certainly regards killing as justified in certain circumstances. I gather he was perfectly prepared to kill Julia and Mr Tambiah when he supposed they had evidence from hollow candles of there being a drug ring in operation.'

'How did he know about our having the candles?' said Theodora to Ian.

'I think he may have been about the evening Julia and I walked up to the asylum. I remember hearing a motorbike engine in the distance.'

'And I suppose if he were trying to track down missing drug candles he could have discovered I had the one from Paul's altar by asking the church warden,' said Theodora. 'He'd know it went missing after my visit. No wonder Jefferson turned over my room.'

'What did Gray suppose he was doing,' the Dean said, with that sudden concentration on administrative detail which marks those responsible for the proper ordering of cathedrals, 'receiving St Manicus candles for use on a parish church's altar? He must have *known* the source was irregular.'

Theodora restrained a smile. It was a long time since the Dean had had to balance the books of a poor parish. If

Jefferson the fixer had told Paul he had a beekeeping friend who could supply cheap candles she doubted if Paul or many another priest would have hesitated for a moment. However, she contented herself with saying, 'I expect Jefferson had a plausible cover story.'

'He must be mad,' said the Archdeacon.

'Actually,' said Theodora, 'with regard to Wheeler's death it's rather difficult to fault him in purely moral terms. It's just that it's more usual to wait until court proceedings have taken their course. Perhaps Jefferson feared that they might not deal justly with Wheeler and of course there is no longer a death penalty. That people should be allowed to drug themselves to death, if they want to and if they haven't the moral stamina to cope with temptation, is less widely held as a view at the present time, but it isn't an incoherent one.'

'How was it managed? Technically, I mean,' asked the Dean.

'I think Jefferson relied on the back door of the office being left open for him and his being apprised of a convenient time.'

'And who did that for him?'

'Oh, no doubt about that,' said Theodora. 'Rosamund Coldharbour. She and Jefferson knew each other from their common work on the PCC of Narborough St Simeon's and Rosamund had finally reached the point of wanting Canon Wheeler to get his comeuppance.'

'Good heavens, why?' said the Archdeacon. 'Why on earth should Miss Coldharbour want Wheeler dead? After all, you don't help to kill someone or anyway abet their being killed just because you have betrayed their secrets.'

The Archdeacon was wrong there, thought Theodora. Given the vagaries of the human heart, you often do wish those you have wronged dead. But before she could frame a reply, Ian broke in. 'When I saw Rosamund on Sunday after the Show, it was clear that she'd been greatly moved by Paul Gray's death. The manner of it horrified her. She'd known him, of course, as a curate at Narborough. She trusted him enough to go to him when she was worried about Wheeler's financial chicanery. Looking back I wonder if she thought those two events were connected, that Wheeler had killed Gray. At the time I just noticed that she showed far more emotion than I'd have thought usual for her.'

'But would she have connived at Jefferson killing Wheeler?' asked the Dean.

'I don't think she'd figured out quite what Jefferson might do,' said Ian. 'She just agreed to see the back door of the office was left open and left the punishment to Jefferson.'

'Wouldn't she fear reprisal if Wheeler came to harm?' asked the Archdeacon.

'I think Rosamund was rather far gone for that.'

'Why?' pursued the Archdeacon.

'That's easy,' Theodora was not too surprised to hear Ian say. 'Rosamund Coldharbour didn't care at all about her own fate or about Canon Wheeler's having had his hand in the till. What she was not prepared to tolerate was a Glaswegian wife of twenty-five years standing. Rosamund, incredibly, loved Charles Wheeler.'

CHAPTER ELEVEN: EARTH OUT OF EARTH IS WONDERFULLY WROUGHT

'O Lord, open thou our lips,' sang the resonant operatic tenor of Canon Sylvester, newly returned from Italy, and indeed, thought Ian, it might almost be La Scala itself.

'And our mouths shall show forth thy praise,' responded Theodora in her pleasant baritone. Seated in her accustomed place at the back of the choir stalls, she allowed her eye to wander up to the high altar and the lancet window of the east end before descending again to the Canons' stalls and the Bishop's throne. Thank Heavens it's all over, she thought happily, and we can resume normal life, that is, Choral Evensong. Then she thought of the Bishop who had lost a son and who could not bear it.

'O Lord, make haste to help us,' the choir answered Canon Sylvester's petition. Ian, a row in front of Theodora, thought of Williams and Mrs Thrigg and the silly collection of half-wits who had come to hate the ordinariness of virtue, the sober and godly life of the Anglican collects, and wanted excitements of a darker kind. What a lot of help we all of us do seem to need.

Julia, sitting between Ian and Dhani, unused to the form of the service, allowed her attention to wander in and out of the words and caught up at 'For there is none other which fighteth for us, but only thou, O Lord.' She thought of her innocent cousin who had become tangled in a net of evil from which he had not had the courage to cut himself free; she thought of Markham, spoilt and contorted in some way now no longer reachable. She thought, I had really better go back to Australia and learn to be a cook or a farm hand. England was too complicated for her.

The petitions ended, the readings and psalms concluded, the splendid spell of the liturgy was almost wound up. The organ ceased. Slowly the Bishop ambled up to the pulpit, following his verger with that peculiar Anglican gait, as though there were all the time in the world, as though the world were owned by and would therefore wait for, the Anglican clergy.

'Our modern derangement,' Julia heard the Bishop say, 'is the same now as in the time of our blessed founder, St Manicus. The madness to which I refer is fear. You will recall our Lord's repeated injunction, often uttered before a miracle of healing, "Fear not".'

Ian thought of Wheeler, who must have spent much of his life being terrified and who sublimated it by bullying. He thought of the Archdeacon's fear which had prevented him from airing his suspicions about the Cathedral and Miss Coldharbour's fear of the knowledge which she had ferreted out. He thought of his own fear of the Bishop which had prevented him speaking out and perhaps saving the Bishop's son.

'Fear and power,' said the Bishop, 'are bound together in our lives. We fear to die, we fear to suffer in our egos more, almost, than in our bodies. Because of that, we are afraid to live. To keep such fears at bay, we seek to make others fear us. It is the only power we have. And yet, my brethren, I beseech you to consider that the icon of true power is the child. Not, that is, the egotistical child of the personality, which leads us back again to demands to be fed with being feared, but the Christ child whose marks are firstly innocence and secondly vulnerability.'

Dhani scrutinised the Bishop's figure. He looked tense round the shoulders, probably suffered from migraine as well as arthritis. He would benefit from a change of diet and a course of body work, thought Dhani compassionately. He could help him. But of course, the Bishop would never dream of either detecting his own illnesses or seeking help from him. Marks of sorrow, marks of woe. Dhani meditated on his own melancholy pleasure at the aptness of the quotation.

'If we are willing,' the Bishop was saying, 'if we can find the strength to suffer, to make ourselves vulnerable even to the wounds which others can inflict on our pride; if we can do this innocently, that is, without hatred or resentment, then we have nothing to fear from fear.'

Theodora thought of Wheeler, whom she needed to pity and forgive. She thought of Jefferson, whose virtue had calloused and grown monstrous. Her eye wandered to the memorial tablet of the seventeenth-century baronet: *Vivit post funera virtus, Goodness survives death.* She prayed, let not evil do the same. Perhaps she had better get in touch with Mrs Wheeler and also see if anything could be done for Miss Coldharbour.

'If we can only draw in,' the Bishop was concluding, 'almost with our breath, almost with our bread, the spirit of truthfulness which comes from prayer and reflection; the spirit of modesty which must come from any appraisal of the self, and the spirit of generosity which can be ours when we contemplate our blessings, then we can surely banish fear and walk as children of light. And now to God the Father, God the Son, and God the Holy Ghost, be ascribed as is most justly due, all might, majesty, dominion and power.'

THE END

THE JOFFE BOOKS STORY

We began in 2014 when Jasper agreed to publish his mum's much-rejected romance novel and it became a bestseller.

Since then we've grown into the largest independent publisher in the UK. We're extremely proud to publish some of the very best writers in the world, including Joy Ellis, Faith Martin, Caro Ramsay, Helen Forrester, Simon Brett and Robert Goddard. Everyone at Joffe Books loves reading and we never forget that it all begins with the magic of an author telling a story.

We are proud to publish talented first-time authors, as well as established writers whose books we love introducing to a new generation of readers.

We have been shortlisted for Independent Publisher of the Year at the British Book Awards three times, in 2020, 2021 and 2022, and for the Diversity and Inclusivity Award at the Independent Publishing Awards in 2022.

We built this company with your help, and we love to hear from you, so please email us about absolutely anything bookish at: feedback@joffebooks.com.

If you want to receive free books every Friday and hear about all our new releases, join our mailing list: www.joffebooks.com/contact.

And when you tell your friends about us, just remember: it's pronounced Joffe as in coffee or toffee!

Printed in Great Britain
by Amazon

18262541R00120